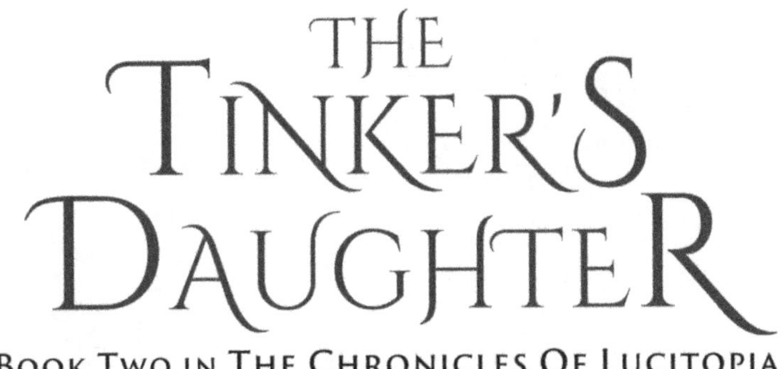

BOOK TWO IN THE CHRONICLES OF LUCITOPIA

JOSEPHINE ANGELINI

LOS ANGELES

ISBN: 979-8-9878321-7-2

Cover by Bianca Sate

Published by Sungrazer Publishing LLC

For my brother Jerry

I

"You don't have to do this, you know," I say.

"Now, now, Jonara," sighs Grieves, the butcher. "My hands are just as tied as yours." We both glance at the iron shackles scraping at my wrists, and at his clearly free ones. I raise a doubtful eyebrow at him. "You know what I mean," he says, soldiering on. "You lost the lottery fair and square."

"Fair and square?" I repeat, just short of shrieking. "My name was the only one in it!"

"It's not our fault you were the only virgin over the asking age of sixteen," Tabbal the tailor rebukes in his smarmy way.

I've always liked Grieves—*always* being the handful of days I've known any of the people in this town—but Tabbal has never been my favorite. Especially since he has tried to relieve me of my virginity on more than one occasion. Unfortunately for him. Being a tinker's adopted daughter, and spending my life traveling from town to town has made me quite good at defending my virginity. Unfortunately for me, I'm now finding out.

"We told you about the dragon when you came to town," Grieves says apologetically.

"But you never told me you were going to *feed* me to it!" I holler back.

Grieves looks over at Ramel, the fat mayor, as if to say that I have a point. Ramel rolls his eyes.

"Look, it's bad luck all around, but we need to give that dragon a sacrifice before he flies down the mountain and burns our village to the ground, yeah?" Ramel says sensibly.

"I thought the lottery was to win a pig!" I say, dumbfounded. "You didn't even bother to tell me I was going to get eaten until *after* we'd been climbing for *three hours*!"

Ramel ignores me and calls over his shoulder to address the torch-bearing mob that has escorted me up this mountain. "Do these shackles attach to the chains on the stake?" he asks anyone at random. He looks at me. "Been almost nine months of this virgin-stringing-up-business, once a month at the full moon like clockwork, and I still don't have the hang of things," he tells me, bouncing on his toes and smiling abashedly at this personal foible of his.

"You don't say," I comment. Unfortunately, my dry wit is lost on him.

Lakonius, the blacksmith, comes forward out of the mob, ducking his head between his hunkering shoulders in shame.

"You do it up like this," he mumbles as he threads a chain dangling from the top of the stake to a big ring on my shackles. I squint meaningfully at Lakonius as he hoists my arms up over my head.

"How many times have I helped you fix something at the forge, Lakonius?" I ask him.

"Sorry, Jonara," he says quietly. "Can fix anything, you can. It's a shame to lose you, but some of us have daughters."

"And I've got a father!" I retort. A thought occurs to me. "Where is he, anyway?"

Lakonius and Grieves share a look. "Well, your father's getting on in years," Grieves replies haltingly.

"He'd never make the climb with that bad back of his," Lakonius adds. "Too much strain for an old man like him."

I look between the two of them. "You didn't tell him, did you? He still thinks I'm getting that pig, doesn't he?" They share a sheepish look. "Unbelievable," I say, turning up my hands. Which is awkward because they are shackled and chained over my head. "This is murder, you know."

"Now, now," Ramel the mayor interjects nervously. He doesn't want any legal entanglements, that's for sure. "The lottery is unbiased."

"It's not a lottery if only one name is in it! You say you've done this nine times already?" I ask, noticing the rig they've got all set up here. "Were all the other victims from out of town as well?"

The mob moves away, leaving me hanging from my shackles. They all take cover behind the giant rocks strewn about the mouth of the enormous cave, before which I am staked. Nothing happens. Time passes and still, nothing happens. My arms have gone numb.

"How do you know he even likes virgins!?" I yell.

"What do you mean? Everyone likes virgins," Ramel, the fat mayor replies.

"Why?" I press.

"Well, you know. They just do." I hear mumbling as he confers with others. "They taste better."

I wonder what happens between a man and a woman that would make a woman's flesh taste bad afterwards. Do men marinate women in something?

"You honestly think that I, lean as I am, taste better than you do?" I ask. "And why only girls? Why not *male* virgins?"

"Because girls aren't as useful as men." I hear Ramel yelp as his wife hits him.

"What would the son of a tinker do that I don't?" I ask.

"He'd fix stuff," Tabbal the tailor says.

"She's better at fixing stuff than her father," Lakonius informs him.

I hear more mumbling.

"A son would carry his father's pack. Right heavy those are," someone—I don't know who—yells out from the darkness.

"I always carry the pack, and it *is* quite heavy," I say. "You've seen my father, haven't you? If he could stand up straight, he'd still be half of me."

"A boy would, you know..." the voice trails off, trying to think what else a boy would do.

My temper slips. I'll admit it: staring into the black mouth of that cave, imagining a dragon coming out of it, is starting to work on my mind. I am not useless, and I deserve to be more than a dragon's dinner.

"Would he keep the house, too!?" I shout into the darkness. "Would a boy get up before his father to prepare breakfast and then spend just as many hours doing just as much if not more work as his father, only to come home, fetch water, chop wood, cook dinner, clean the laundry, do the dishes, sweep the floors, and finally go to bed four hours after his father's been sleeping, only to get up an hour before him to do it all over again!? Hmm? Would a boy do that!? Come to think of it, why am I even fighting this whole getting eaten by a dragon business!?"

"Exactly! Why are you fighting it? The other girls had stopped crying by now."

"I'm not crying!" I snap. "I'm pointing out that there are grave injustices in both the distribution of labor and the expectations that society places on women."

There's a pause. "Well, *stop* it. You'll give the other women funny ideas."

I sigh deeply, and we all wait some more. Some of the townspeople have started back down the mountain, grumbling about an early start in the morning. Nice to know my death is so boring they can't be bothered to wait for the climax. My arms are all pins and needles. If it was going to take this long, they could've made it more comfortable. They could have tied me to a chair, or something. The stake is pure theatrics at this point.

A thought occurs to me. "Why haven't any of you tried killing the dragon?" I ask.

"Why would we do that?" the unknown voice responds. "The dragon's the only thing keeping the bandits away."

There have been an awful lot of bandits about since the old king died with no heir, and some upstart sorcerer started challenging all the peacekeeping knights to single combat. Asphodel is the sorcerer's name and blasts it if he doesn't keep winning. There are practically no knights left.

"Why don't you hire the bandits to *kill* the dragon, then?" I suggest. "Times are tough, you know. Most of the bandits I've encountered on the roads are only dabbling in banditry because they are in need of gainful employment."

And a lot of them are starting to join up with Asphodel. He's building a bloody army. Won't be safe on the roads any more for Da and me. Not that I am going to be doing much walking about, presently, as it seems I am to become some dragon's dinner. Unbelievable.

I hear more whispering. I believe someone says that virgins are cheaper. I'm working myself up to a decent-sized rage when I hear something coming from the cave.

There is a great rumble and a gust of dry, burnt air belches out around me, blowing my white dress and my unbound hair back in such a forceful gust that my eyes water. I hear the hidden townsfolk scream and the sounds of them scrambling to get farther away.

From the darkness, there is a scraping sound and a giant *sniff*. I feel the air around me getting sucked toward the mouth of the cave. There's another scraping sound and a scaly claw, each talon longer than my body, comes into view. Then, the tip of an enormous golden snout appears over the claw and two green eyes glow in the darkness. The rest of the dragon's face still hidden in the gloom.

Bollox.

My whole life I did everything right. I kept my head down, I did my work, and now I'm going to die because of it.

I know that at twenty I'm quite old for marriage and that any halfway decent village girl is usually betrothed by the time she's fifteen, but there were plenty of boys (okay, maybe just one) who had shown interest in marrying me. I'm no great beauty, but neither was he, and I've got skills, hang it all.

But I didn't even let him court me because that would have meant that I'd have to leave my poor father—who, honestly?—is a terrible tinker. Couldn't fix a nail to a board with a hammer, that one. Actually, I never trusted him with the hammers. Mostly, I just let him drink tea with the customers and keep them entertained while I got down to the business of fixing things. Very entertaining, my da. Stories are his life. He's got a story about everything, and he's fantastic at telling them.

Storytelling isn't very lucrative. But I stuck with my adopted father because he took me in as a babe and taught me everything he knew. Then I figured out the rest on my own when I realized that he didn't really know very much. He did teach me to read and do arithmetic, which has been quite useful, though I've had to explain to him on many occasions that zero coins equals *zero* food. He hasn't quite understood that subtlety in mathematics just yet.

Still, I love my da. But that's not the only reason I've stuck by him. It's the principle of the thing. You don't leave a kind old man who took you in as a child, just because an enterprising young man says he likes the look of your ankles. Which wasn't even a very good compliment, come to think of it. No, if I'm going to abandon my aged benefactor and earn a living for some other man, it's going to be for one who can come up with something better to talk about than the first body part he happens to look down and see.

Maybe it's just the hot breath of doom stirring my blood, but I've suddenly decided that I want poetry, dammit. Love. As hard as I've worked, I deserve some of that romance my father is always spinning yarns about. Failing that, I definitely *don't* deserve to get eaten by a bloody dragon—but apparently that's what's going to happen because that's what I get for being a good girl. Ruddy bastards, the lot of them. Especially that blasted dragon.

"Well, what are you waiting for, you big lummox!?" I shout at the green eyes hovering over the golden snout. "Go ahead and eat me, and may you choke on my bones!"

I hear the few remaining townspeople gasp from behind their rocks.

The great head of the dragon finally emerges from the mouth of the cave. His scales twinkle like oiled gold. His big, liquid eyes are pools of pure emerald with a dot of inky black in the center. The sharp teeth showing along the edge of his lower lip are ivory white, except for the left canine. That tooth is a spike of diamond, longer than my leg. I gasp. I can't help it. He's more gorgeous than the dawn.

"Wow. You're beautiful," I say, mesmerized.

He snorts smoke and rumbles, breaking my momentary reverie. My legs start to shake in panic. Until now I was too angry about being duped to feel much of anything, but it occurs to me that I could quite possibly be *eaten*. What a horrible way to die.

One of his claws reaches out for me and I scream. I scramble around to the other side of the pole, barely evading him. He snatches at me again and I use the chains to hoist myself up over his scaly grasp. Carrying that tinker's pack from town to town has made me heartier than most girls.

"Ha!" I yell, emboldened by my small victory, though my voice quavers with a healthy dose of terror. "I can do this all night!"

Dragon jerks back and puffs hot air through his nostrils, as if surprised. He leans down again, one of his emerald eyes peering closely at me. His eye is as big as I am. I scurry behind the stake, keeping low and feinting left and right in an asinine attempt to keep him guessing. My options for concealment are... limited. He peers at me curiously, not like a ravening beast at all. Though I may be a fool for it, I can't feel as frightened of him as I probably should be. If he smelled like carrion, or if there were carcasses strewn about, I'd certainly be able to muster up the requisite shock and horror, but this lair of his is quite tidy. Nary a skull in sight.

"I promise, I'm not worth the effort, Dragon," I call out, offering a truce. "You'll work up a bigger hunger trying to catch me than eating me could ever slake."

Dragon reaches again, and though I dodge him, he's too fast for me. He catches me by my leg and pulls. But of course, I'm chained to the stake. I stop short and scream with the pain of being nearly torn in two. Dragon drops me at the sound of my distress, and I slam against the stake. My head explodes and my vision blurs. I blink my eyes, trying to remain conscious, and see him reaching for me again. This time he grasps me around the waist, dare I say... carefully? He tugs on me a few times in an exploratory way. He's not trying to hurt me, but it still feels like my arms are getting yanked out of the sockets.

"I'm *attached* to it, you glittering oaf!" I holler, pointing to the stake.

He makes a rumbling sound deep in his throat, and maybe it's just the knock I took to the head, but it sounds like he's laughing. Dragon easily plucks the stake out of the ground and gathers me and the stake into one of his front claws. As his talons close to form a cage around me, I capitulate to the swirling feeling in my head and everything goes black.

2

I'm aware of the pain first, then the sound of flowing water.

I have to convince myself not to fall back to sleep no matter how hard it is to stay awake. I hit my head quite hard, and I know that sleeping after a blow to the head can mean death. In the last few years, I've seen many head wounds as the byways have become more treacherous and banditry abounds. I've learned much of healing since the name *Asphodel* began to be whispered in taverns not two years ago.

I know I must open my eyes, even though my head is splitting, or else I may never open them again. But sleep beckons.

I hear a deep rumbling sound. Like a dragon. My eyes pop open. I am now fully awake.

Dragon has his head resting next to mine. One of his giant eyes is peering at me, half shut. He rumbles again, and I sit up, kicking myself away from him. Gold coins and jewels fly up from under my feet. My chains jangle and clank among them until they stop me short. I'm still attached to the stake, and though Dragon pulled it from the ground as easily as I would a blade of grass, I can't even make the thick pole budge an inch.

He doesn't lunge after me. He isn't salivating, as far as I can see. When my breathing finally settles down, I cautiously accept that Dragon has no plans to eat me. At least for now.

When I'm sufficiently convinced of this—and equally confused by it—I risk peeling my gaze away from Dragon long enough to have a look around.

A soft light suffuses the cave, but I can't locate the origin. Everything around me sparkles and amplifies the light, bouncing it around and refracting it in prisms. I put my hands down among the dragon hoard. Rubies, opals, and amethysts spill through my fingers. Emeralds, topaz, and sapphires slip under my bare feet. I gaze further. Dragon and I sit atop a heap of gold and jewels larger than the biggest house in the village.

A dark, still pool of water lies at the edge of the hoard. The trickling sound I hear comes from the walls, which run with crystal-clear melt water from the mountaintop piled above us. I can't see the mouth of the cave and I still can't tell where the light is coming from. I wonder how deep inside the mountain we are.

I look at Dragon suspiciously. "Why haven't you eaten me?" I ask him.

He puffs hot air through his nostrils in answer.

"Are you saving me for later?"

He rumbles deep in his chest. Almost like he's saying

maybe. I can't help it—I laugh. I realize I am not afraid of him. In fact, after that first moment of abject terror when he reached for me, I don't think I ever fully squared with the notion that he was going to eat me. Something about the utter lack of bloodlust in his eyes told me I was about as palatable to him as a hedgehog would be to me.

"Well, while you're deciding, I'd like to take these chains off. They hurt."

Now that I may take a good look at my bonds, I can see that the shackles are held together by a peaked pin. To remove the pin, all one needs to do is rotate it in the correct pattern through the hasps. Not too hard for anyone to do, really, and for me it's child's play. Devising locks to safeguard a town's treasures, and even for some of the wealthier people's personal use, has become something of a specialty of mine in this age of mounting lawlessness. This land is in dire need of a king. Anyone, really, who can stand up to Asphodel and his growing army of bandits.

I twist and pull, twist again, and withdraw the pin. The shackle on one wrist falls open and I look at the skin under it, rubbed red and raw.

"Well, I suppose there's no need to go about devising a warded lock to use on a frantic girl," I say, insulted. And chagrined. "I could have gotten out of these as we climbed the mountain, but I didn't think about getting away. I was too..." I break off, not knowing what I had been, and look up at Dragon's hooded eye. "No one even tried to stop it," I say because it seems like he's waiting for me to finish. "It's like I don't even matter."

My face gets hot. Rather than cry, I look down at the second shackle and work the pin out of the hasps in stages.

"It's not like I expected anyone to throw themselves in front of me and offer themselves up in my place, but no one even questioned it."

I wipe my face. I can't believe I'm crying in front of Dragon, but I'm sure he's seen his fair share of weeping women. He's probably confused as to why I haven't cried yet.

"What did I expect?" I say, letting the tears flow. "After a lifetime of traveling from town to town, did I suddenly think that this was going to be the place where I found a home?"

The second shackle falls open, exposing my other wrist. It's worse off, and bleeding.

I feel Dragon's hot breath on my arm and look, startled that he's so close to me. His forked tongue snakes out and licks his diamond tooth.

"Oh, *now* you're going to eat me?" I say, sniffling and crying. I hold out my bloody wrist. "Go ahead. You can't hurt me worse than they have."

Dragon refuses my offer. Instead, he rumbles and rises. And he keeps rising. Suddenly, there is a *lot* of dragon looking down at me. He unfurls his red-golden wings, and I belatedly realize that he has them. They curve over me like the sails of an enormous ship. Through the membrane-thin triangles of skin are veins of bone, and ridged along the bottom of the wings, talons of solid gold stick out like fangs. He flaps his wings and spins onto the back of his long, spiked tail. Dragon raises one of his hind legs and scratches at his long neck.

A shower of gold coins and jewels spills like rain from

between Dragon's scales. I roll away before any of them can knock my already damaged head. He bellows and huffs and scratches harder and harder. Then he trumpets in frustration and nearly shatters my aching skull with the sound of it.

"All right, all right!" I yell, covering my ears. "Lie down so I may climb up your back and take a look at what's bothering you."

Dragon pauses and huffs through his nose.

"Lie down so I may climb up," I repeat, gesturing with my hands as I speak. Surprisingly, he does as I ask.

There's no easy way up to where Dragon was trying to scratch. He was reaching for a spot on his shoulder blades that lies between his massive wings, and, even folded, the wings are in the way.

I decide the best path up Dragon is to climb over his foreleg and see if I can hoist myself along his neck somehow. I step onto the back of Dragon's front claw and crouch down, using my hands to steady myself. Before I can find a way to crawl onto his back, Dragon lifts his foreleg and puts me level with his neck.

"That's lovely," I tell him, and from there I easily swing myself astride his neck, just in front of his wings. I sit tall, heels down. "Like riding a very fat horse," I remark.

Dragon rumbles at me and cocks his head back a bit to glare at me with a big eye.

"I'm not calling *you* fat, but your neck is very wide for my legs to go 'round." I swivel my hips, feeling the large, golden scales under my seat. "But this spot on you is almost like a saddle, really. You're quite comfortable, Dragon."

He rumbles again, this time sounding more impatient.

"Fine, I'm going. The itchy spot was down between your wings, yes?" I ask, though I don't know why. It's not like he's going to answer me.

Dragon holds still as I crawl on hands and knees down his spine. A few feet in front of me I can see that some of his scales are not lying completely flat against his body.

"I'll have to stick my hand under there," I warn him. "If you don't like it, I'm sure you'll just incinerate me."

I slide my hand under Dragon's scales and feel all kinds of hard, sharp lumps embedded in the skin beneath. As soon as I touch the inflamed lumps, Dragon's hind leg starts scratching uselessly at the air, like a dog when you rub it behind the ears.

Though it's somewhat off-putting, I start scratching. I feel the hard lumps easily pop out of the skin. Dragon rumbles with satisfaction, and since I know I'm not hurting him, I dig in with relish.

You know how it is when you start working out some kind of splinter or blemish or boil. It's revolting, but you can't seem to quit until you get all of it. Whatever this is, it doesn't smell infected. In fact, it smells like Dragon, which is a spicy, smoky scent—dry and clean—that I find immensely pleasing. When I've dislodged the lumps, I must reach with my whole arm to scoop them out because there are veritable baskets full under there.

Though they're unaccountably heavy I'm still expecting a pimple-like extrusion, yet instead, what I haul out are exquisitely carved jewels the size of my eye and gold coins that gleam as if newly minted. As Dragon sighs with relief, I stare at one of the coins in amazement. Embossed on one side of it is the image of a dragon, and on the other is a knight.

"This one coin of solid gold is more wealth than I've managed to scrape together in my entire life," I say musingly. "And you produce it under your skin like a teenager produces spots."

I laugh as I push the coin and the rest of the precious items off Dragon's back, so they may join the entirety of his hoard.

"I'll never look at riches the same way again, that's for sure," I say as I crawl back up Dragon's neck and to his waiting foreleg.

He balances me on the back of one claw long enough to scoop me up in the other. Dragon holds me, comfortably leaning back against the digits of his cupped claw as he draws me level with his eyes. I perch my elbows on the top edge of his fist as he and I regard each other.

"I'll scratch your back if you don't eat me," I tell him. "I think it's a fairly good bargain, considering I'm hardly a meal for a grown dragon like you." My stomach growls. "Speaking of which, what do you eat when you're not devouring virgins?"

Dragon cocks his head and narrows his eyes like he's trying to understand me.

I open my mouth and point down my throat. Then I rub my belly emphatically. "I'm hungry. I need to eat. If you've got nothing here, you *could* just let me go," I try.

Dragon rumbles and smoke puffs out his nostrils. In one great bound he jumps over the hoard, soars through the air—

all with me caged securely behind his talons—and plunges into the black, icy water of the pool.

3

I can't say for certain how long we are submerged.

Too long, is what my burning lungs tell me. By the time we break through to the air again, I am gasping and choking spasmodically. I brace myself against Dragon's talons and hack away. I assume he swims us to shore as I nearly expel an internal organ because when I finally stop coughing, I find that I am on my hands and knees in the greenest grass I've ever seen.

I sit back on my heels and look around as I wipe my streaming eyes. Dragon is lying next to me with his head down on his paws, his face level with my body. He's watching me. His cat-like eyes are rounded with worry, and he makes a noise that is half purr, half whimper.

"I'm all right, Dragon," I say, though my voice is raspy, and my teeth are chattering with the cold. "But next time, please try to remember that I can't hold my breath as long as you can."

He rumbles in response. I reach out and rub his snout. It's warm to the touch, though the water we were in was so cold my fingertips are blanched.

"This place is absolutely stunning," I say, taking in the pristine alpine meadow rolled out in front of me. The lake is a pearly blue. The grass is spotted with lacy flowers. The distance is filled with snow-capped mountains.

Just behind the lake is a tall peak. I point to it.

"Is that your mountain, Dragon?" I ask. I cock my head at the semi-circular lake, imagining how its other shore must be under the mountain, lapping against Dragon's hoard.

His enormous head rises and keeps rising until he is sitting up with his wings unfurled. He glitters in the sun for a breathtaking moment, and then he springs into the sky. His wings push the air down, nearly flattening me with the force of it as he climbs gracefully upward. Almost immediately he pivots back downward and arrows into the lake with his wings folded against his body.

For such a colossal creature, he barely makes a splash.

As the minutes pass, the small waves made by Dragon's body turn to ripples, and then the ripples subside back into a glassy calm.

I go to the edge of the lake. "Dragon?" I call out. I peer into the milky blue of the water but see nothing. "Dragon!" I yell.

I wrap my arms around me. The white smock and kirtle I wore to my own virgin sacrifice are barely sufficient to keep me warm when they're bone dry. Wet, they're about as functional as wearing cobwebs. I didn't notice with Dragon nearby. He's so warm.

Did he leave me, and if he did, what do I do now? I could run away! This is my chance to escape! If I cross the meadow and make it back to the mountain, I could try to find a pass across it, and if I do that, I could possibly make it back to the village... never. I'd never make it all the way up over the mountain and back to the village before Dragon found me. And then he'd eat me for sure, wouldn't he?

It also occurs to me that if I run back to the village (that's if I could climb over a mountain without getting spotted by Dragon in the first place) they'll know I got away from him somehow. They'll force me up the mountain again, assuming Dragon will be angry if they don't give me back to him, and they could be right. If I run away leaving them with no virgin sacrifice Dragon might be angry enough to kill them all. Including my Da.

But if I run and I *don't* go back to the village, where will I go? Without my father, I'm just a woman alone. Unemployable. And what will happen to my father? He's even more unemployable than I am—and that's assuming he manages to survive the destruction of the town if Dragon decides to be wrathful.

But as the moments pass, I realize I was never really considering running, and not because of the possible consequences. I was *given* to Dragon. Against my will, yes, but I've gotten past that part. The whole virgin sacrifice thing is rather like a wedding, now that I consider it. There's a white dress, the whole town shows up, and there are rings involved, though mine were shackles. That's not the point. I was given to him, and he didn't want me. I'm sure he went ahead and gobbled up all the other virgins they threw at him, but he leaves me, half-drowned and freezing cold, on the wrong side of the mountain.

"Dragon!" I shout, angry now.

I sigh as his golden head rises above the surface of the water. He streams toward me in a V, his sinuous backbone snaking across the glassy surface and his nostrils puffing steam. I manage to smile at him as he comes to shore, but I'm still upset.

"You took a long time," I scold. "I thought you'd left me."

He walks around me, nudging me with his nose, as if I'm not in the right place. I let him bump me until we are back on the grass again, and he opens his mouth.

Dozens, maybe tens of dozens of fish pour out from between his teeth. Most of them are still flapping. I laugh at the embarrassment of riches laid before me.

"I did tell you I was hungry," I admit, grinning. "Thank you, Dragon. But I hope you're planning on eating most of this, as I only require one."

I pick out a decent-sized fish, but I have no knife to gut and clean it. I look around for something suitable, but the only things sharp and pointy enough are attached to Dragon. I could try to ask him to gut the fish for me, but his talons are much too thick to make a decent job of it. There are a few spikes at the end of his tail that look promising, though.

I go to his tail and touch one of the smaller spikes. It immediately pricks my finger and draws blood. I suck in a breath and hear Dragon rumble. I glance up at him and see that he's watching me.

"I need a knife," I tell him, holding up my fish. I draw my other hand across the middle of the fish as if I'm cutting it.

I hear something tumble onto the grass, look down, a realize that the spike I'd just touched has fallen out of Dragon's tail. I stoop down and inspect it. The part of the spike that was stuck inside Dragon is white, and it looks almost exactly like a grip. I touch it warily, thinking it might cut me, but it is as smooth and rounded as a tooth. I heft it in my hand. It's so light. I grasp the fish in my other hand lengthwise and slit it right up the belly without feeling one tug. I know a thing or two about tools, and this is not only the sharpest edge I've ever encountered, but also the lightest and the most elegant-looking blade I've ever seen.

"This is the finest object I've ever held in my hand," I tell Dragon appreciatively.

He makes a proud sound and buries his snout in the pile of fish. When I'm finished gutting and cleaning my fish, I wash the blade in the lake and bring it back to Dragon's tail. The hole it came out of is bleeding. I try to fit it back in, but Dragon moves his tail away. I walk over and try again, and again Dragon repositions himself.

"Hold still," I tell him. "I'm trying to put it back."

He huffs hot air out of his nose and wraps his tail under his body stubbornly.

I look at the blade in my hand. The jewels and coins I saw pouring out of Dragon's body were precious, but this blade is past wealth. And he bleeds for it.

"You need to let me try to put this back in you," I tell him. "It's left a hole."

He *snaps* at me. I'm so shocked I don't know what to do

for a moment. I stare at him, mouth agape, until he drops his great head onto his front talons contritely.

"Do you truly mean for me to keep this?" I ask carefully.

Dragon makes a pleased purring sound.

"I can't take this," I tell him. "It's too fine."

He growls and tucks his tail tighter to his body.

I look down at the thing of beauty in my hand. It's a dark metal, almost as if some alchemist had learned how to smelt mercury and onyx together. The blade is three-quarters the length of my forearm and nearly the exact same width of it. It is shaped long and tapering like a willow leaf, and a wave snakes up the center of the blade. The grip is exactly three fingers longer than my clasped fist, and it is made of smooth, white bone.

I look back up at Dragon. "I will watch over this for you, but I cannot keep it," I tell him. "I am honored that you have loaned me..." I feel I must name this piece of Dragon, and I search my mind for something proper, but not frilly. "I am honored to carry Dragonbarb, and I will return it to you when you see fit."

Dragon huffs smoke out of his nostrils in agreement.

He's finished all the fish save the one I'm holding. The smoke coming out of his nose gives me an idea. I have no sheath for Dragonbarb, so I must sheath it in the earth, white grip sticking up, or I could injure myself on it accidentally. I go down to the edge of the lake and gather some flat rocks of equal width, lay them alongside each other, and put the flayed fish on top.

"Will you cook that for me?" I ask Dragon. He cocks his head in question, his big emerald eyes unblinking. "Breathe fire," I say. I bend down over my fish and breathe on it. Then I point up at Dragon.

He makes a confused mewling sound.

"I'll stand back," I say. "Just do that," I say, breathing out and swooping my arms wide in what is probably a ridiculous pantomime of breathing fire. "On that." I point back down at the fish.

I see a tendril of fire escape from between Dragon's lips.

"Yes, that!" I say, jumping up and down. "Do that on the fish!"

A great gout of fire spills over my little fish like a mountain of lava overturned. I can smell the char after one second and realize my folly.

"Stop, Dragon!" I holler, and he does.

We both look down at the cinder that was my fish. Dragon makes a grumbly growly noise.

"I know, you tried to tell me. Is there any way you could do a tiny flame?" I ask, holding two fingers up a mere inch apart to indicate something small.

Dragon pads away from me. He slips into the water, snakes across the surface for a few lengths, and then disappears without a sound or a ripple.

"Lovely," I say, sitting down on the grass. But he isn't gone long this time.

When Dragon returns, he canters up from the lake dripping water and lays a single, perfect, very large fish at my feet. It's more food than I can eat in two days, but I smile and thank him. I gut the fish, clean the ash off my ledge of flat rocks, and lay the freshly flayed fish on top.

"Just a little flame?" I ask Dragon.

He obliges and gently sears my fish with his hot breath. I look at the crisped skin, dark brown but not black, and smell the sizzling fat.

"I wish I had some salt," I say, pinching a piece of flesh between my fingers and scalding them a little. I don't care, though. I am so hungry by now that I eat until my belly feels tight.

Dragon lies down behind me, his great head resting in the grass, and I lean back against his neck while I eat. When I'm finished, I go down to the lake to wash up, taking extra care with my raw wrists, before re-joining Dragon.

I lie back against him, feeling warm and full. His front claw reaches up and wraps around me and I fall asleep, cupped in his hand.

4

I wake before dawn to find Dragon staring at me, his eyes half closed.

I stretch and yawn, groggy after my long sleep. I notice his claw lying next to me, and though it encased me from head to toe with ease a few hours ago, now it appears no bigger than half of me.

"Dragon, have you shrunk?" I ask him.

He stands and stretches, unfurling his wings and reaching his long neck. His jaws open wide to reveal hundreds of dagger-like teeth, some serrated, and a red forked tongue that unwinds ribbon-like and lolls between them. When he's done stretching, and shedding a few coins here and there, he seems to be back to his full stature. Curious.

"Are we returning to the mountain now?" I ask, pulling Dragonbarb out of the ground. "Because if we are, might I suggest we—"

Dragon suddenly scoops me up in his claw, jumps into

the air, and arrows back down at the lake. I know what's coming this time. I hold Dragonbarb by the hilt securely, careful to keep it away from my body and take the deepest breath I can manage while we are still airborne. I tell myself to relax, but the cold is such a shock it seems to shrink my lungs.

I try not to panic when we enter an underwater cave, and everything goes too dark for me to see. I count instead, but when the number becomes alarmingly high, I decide panicking is perfectly acceptable at this juncture.

As soon as I feel us break the surface, I sputter and cough after nearly drowning for the second time in a day. I suppose it's a bit better this time, though it's still rather awful. Dragon places me on top of his hoard and watches me, mewling contritely and prodding me with his snout every now and again, until I've caught my breath. I am careful to put Dragonbarb blade down into the hoard, so I don't cut myself on it while I wheeze and flop about.

"*Fly*," I gasp, finishing my original thought. "Might I suggest we *fly* from now on?" I point to Dragon's wings and flap my arms. "You know, fly up here. I can ride you or you can carry me in your talons. Either's fine with me. But no more lake." Dragon looks over at the water's edge while I cough a few more times. "I don't want to go under there again, thank you."

Dragon rumbles and puts his head down on his front claws like he understands.

My Da told me many stories of magical creatures over the years. Always loved a good story, my da. Trouble was, I never knew which of his stories were real and which were made up.

Dragons were one of his favorite topics, he certainly loved talking about dragons more than tinkering. Out of boredom or frustration or sheer pig-headedness, I ignored all dragon stories assiduously over the years and now I wish I'd listened to them. Not that my da ever troubled himself to get his facts straight. Everything was a story to my da, subject to change as fancy struck him, even things that I knew were cold, hard reality. I regard Dragon, my head tilted to the side as I try to figure him out.

"You're very clever, aren't you?" I ask him.

He tilts *his* head to the side as if to mirror me, and then he puffs smoke out of his nose clownishly, making me laugh.

"You're cheeky, too." I shiver and move closer to his ever-warm body.

He picks me up in one of his claws and breathes hot air over me until I stop shaking. Then, he rumbles and rolls over onto his back. I see some scales on his underbelly bubbling up as they did between his wings when jewels had formed under them.

"You want me to scratch your belly?" I ask. He hums deep inside, making his belly vibrate. "Yes, I will. But you must do something for me after." He makes a musing noise that I take to be a yes, and I crawl onto his pale golden underside.

His scales are longer and thinner here. They are softer to the touch as well. His belly flutters as I run my hands over him, and he makes a sound almost like laughing. For a moment, I am aware of how strange this is. I can't believe I'm tickling a dragon. But then I get back to business and crawl down to the scales that don't lie flat. I stick my arm under them and give him a good scratch, excoriating a king's ransom in the process.

I climb down and brush off my hands, which are covered in gold dust. It sparkles in the air all around, floating like fairy wishes.

"Now, you must help me, Dragon," I announce. I walk down to the edge of the lake and start gathering stones. "I need you to build me a well on the edge of this lake. Go on. Get in the water."

Following the motion of my hand, Dragon slides into the lake, his sinuous body snaking just under the black surface. When he surfaces and faces me, I start dropping rocks down in a semicircle along a six or seven-foot-deep edge of the lake.

"I'm building a well on the side of this lake, but I need help. Can you bring more rocks and shore up this little area under the surface?"

Dragon stares at me for a while. I keep blocking off a small section and I let him watch me do it until he sinks silently beneath the surface. Though I can only see flashes of his golden body under the clear dark water, I can tell he is following my instructions. Staying submerged while he places rocks atop each other, Dragon blocks off a pool for me from the rest of the lake.

I risk the life-threatening cold and jump into my walled-off well of water to shore up the top. Then I haul myself out and, shivering, I huddle close to Dragon's warmth.

I clasp tightly to his hot foreleg and look up at him. "Breathe fire on it, Dragon."

Dragon lowers his snout close to the section of walled-off water and blasts it with his dragon flame. In moments I see the water glow and boil. Hot steam erupts around Dragon's face. He dips his head into the water, and I see him flame even though he's beneath the surface.

"Stop," I tell him, tapping on his foreleg. The flame abates, and he lifts his head out of the water.

Steam rises from the top of the small pool. I sidle up to it and risk a toe. It is, as expected, scalding hot. But the perfect temperature to clean my clothes.

I strip down hastily. I don't dare put my hand into water this temperature, but I get Dragon to dip my smock, kirtle, and undergarments into the boiling water with his claw. When I've directed him to dunk them a sufficient number of times, I let them cool in his claw for a while before I hazard wringing them out and laying them atop his hoard.

"Well, they'll be dusted in gold for drying here, and all the lovelier for it, probably," I say, bracing my fists on my bare hips and smiling up at Dragon. He drops his head down and nuzzles me with his snout, nearly knocking me over. I grab onto him and laugh as he rubs his smoky, spicy hide against me, leaving his perfume all over me.

"Thank you, Dragon, that smells lovely," I say, holding his snout and looking into his big green eyes. "But I still need a bath."

I turn to my pool and work my way into the hot water an inch at a time. Dragon lays his chin down on the edge, his snout bubbling in the water next to me as I stretch myself out, floating on the surface. I lay one arm across Dragon's nose and lie back, letting my head go. My ears are under the surface, my limbs floating.

The only thing tarnishing this moment of utter bliss is

the sting of the cuts left on my wrists from the shackles. They are still too tender to let me fully enjoy this moment. Yet, even as I notice this, Dragon breathes out and blows bubbles in the water through his teeth. The effervescent feeling is such a relief I no longer feel an ache or sting in any muscle or cut. I giggle and roll in the bubbling water.

Dragon edges his snout under me, and I half-lie, half-float on top of his long nose, stretched out with the warm water over me and under me in two thin sheets. It feels like I'm under a blanket that presses down comfortingly, while at the same time, I'm floating on top of a cloud. Dragon's nostrils, peaking just above the surface, breathe warm, smoky air over my exposed toe-tips.

I don't think I sleep. I am too in awe of how perfect this moment is to relinquish this feeling to oblivion, but I'm near sleep when I feel Dragon startle and stiffen.

I raise my head and roll off his snout into the pool. "What is it?" I ask him, kicking my way to the shore.

While I'm climbing out, I hear human voices echoing from the entrance. I creep toward the source of the sound, and Dragon rumbles low behind me. I turn and gesture emphatically for him to be quiet. He hunkers down and slinks along behind me.

As I climb upward among stalactites and stalagmites of white limestone toward the sound, I notice that I'm moving toward daylight and slightly fresher air. I stop and hide behind a large boulder before I get to the mouth of the cave. There are two men and a boy out there with tools. After I get a glimpse of their faces, I stay completely behind the boulder and settle for simply listening in on their conversation, rather than watching. I don't want to risk them finding me.

"Never seen him take the whole stake before," Lakonius, the blacksmith, is saying.

"I never seen him take anything," says another voice I don't know.

"What do you mean, Da?" asks the boy.

"Just that. We've never seen him take a girl, though we've waited and watched," the boy's father replies. "We'll have to put the new stake over here. The ground's not firm enough there."

"He might have taken some of the girls," Lakonius argues.

"I've never seen him do it." I hear digging. "And more than one girl has wandered down the mountain saying he never showed up."

"Just two. What about the other girls?" Lakonius asks. "We've never found a skeleton hanging from the post, either."

The father, who I'm assuming is a carpenter, makes a guffawing sound. "Those girls got out of the chains and ran away, they did. And who'd blame them after the whole town tried to feed them to a dragon."

"If he doesn't eat them, why do we keep leaving girls up here?" the boy asks.

"Terrible things happen if you don't leave a sacrifice for a dragon," Lakonius says in a fell voice.

"Ya," agrees the carpenter. "This dragon came from the north. Do you see that mountain there?"

"What?" The boy sniggers. "The one that looks like a pecker?"

"Watch it, boy," his father says in warning. Then, I hear all three of them break into laughter for a moment before they remind each other this is serious business and settle down.

"The town beneath that mountain—"

"What's it called? Bolloxville?" the boy guesses.

"Er—yes, actually," Lakonius replies. Another round of laughter.

"It's not funny," the carpenter says, although I can hear his laugh mixed in with theirs. "Not like this town has a better name."

"What happened in... Bolloxville?" the boy asks, mumbling the name to repress another round of laughter.

The group grows quiet for too long.

"They're cursed, they are," the carpenter replies.

"They didn't leave a sacrifice for the dragon," Lakonius says warningly. "Doesn't matter if he doesn't eat it. It's the leaving that counts."

"No. That was Asphodel that cursed them," the carpenter says, disagreeing.

I hear Dragon rumble menacingly behind me and I turn to shush him.

"Never in your life," Lakonius argues. "They didn't leave a proper virgin sacrifice for the new dragon."

"And the dragon cursed them?" the carpenter scoffs disbelievingly. "Dragons burn villages, they don't cast spells. Sorcerers do that, only no one knows about it properly because there've been no minstrels to bring the news."

"Aye. That I have noticed," Lakonius says in a heavy tone. "No word from anyone these days. No news, nary a player nor juggler in town squares hailing from the north."

I think back on it, and it's true. Da and I have come up from the south this past year and the farther north we've gotten, the fewer minstrels we've seen. In fact, I can't recall having seen *any* in half a year.

"It's the north that Asphodel's cursed," the carpenter says.

"How are they cursed?" the boy asks.

"Don't rightly know," his father replies. "And I don't want to know. You keep out of this, and anything having to do with Asphodel, do you hear me?"

"I hear you, Da," the boy says.

"Right, then. We should be off before we lose the light," Lakonius says.

"We'll leave this lot here so as not to be carrying it up and down the mountain, and come back with some more men and the post," the carpenter replies, his voice growing distant as they move away. "We'll have it ready by the next full moon."

When I'm sure they're gone, I come out. As soon as I'm about to leave the cave, I feel Dragon's claw wrap around me. He picks me up and looks at me.

"What are you doing?" I ask him.

He makes a mewling noise.

"It's all right. The men are gone."

His big green eyes are still rounded with worry.

"Did you think I was going to leave you? Well, I wasn't.

Certainly not without a stitch of clothing on my body. Now put me down so I may have a look around."

Dragon obliges, and I go outside to find that the carpenter has left his tools and the blacksmith has left his chains. I feel like kicking the ruddy chains down the mountain, but I know that's silly. Instead, I go through the carpenter's tool satchel. He's got quite a nice collection, honestly.

"I think I sold him this awl," I tell Dragon, holding it up.

Dragon rumbles—and I get the impression he's just shrugged as if to tell me he wouldn't know an awl from a goat.

"Well, it's a nice one," I inform Dragon, slipping the awl back into its loop on one of the three stiff leather boards inside the satchel.

I'm no thief. But I need this kit more than the carpenter does. I look at Dragon and narrow my eyes.

"Will you loan me some coin?" I ask him.

Dragon makes a questioning sound.

"Come here," I tell him, "I want to scratch behind your jaw."

I reach up and make the gesture for scratching, and he eagerly lowers his head. I itch out a few gold coins from behind the twisted spikes of gold that flare back, antler-like, from Dragon's head. He sighs deeply and closes his eyes while I work my way around his jawbone. I pull out an opal and an amethyst as well, but these I think I should bring back to the hoard.

"Thank you, Dragon," I tell him, leaving behind two pieces of gold worth twenty tool kits, while I take up the carpenter's satchel. Dragon follows me as I go back into his cave. "I only hope I can find a way to fashion a sheath for Dragonbarb with these."

I spend the rest of the day looking for discarded dragon scales. I only find a couple that are from his back, and not the softer, penetrable ones on his underbelly. The hard dragon scales are far rarer than jewels, that's for sure, and once I start testing one of them with my newly purchased tools, I begin to understand why. The only thing that can cut them is Dragonbarb, and even then, it isn't easy.

After I've finally managed to fashion a rudimentary sheath for Dragonbarb and stow it, now slightly more safely, in the satchel, I look up at Dragon and rub the sweat off my brow.

"I don't suppose you'd be inclined to heat up my bath for me again, would you?"

He's been watching me for some time through drooping lids. I walk over to my pool and touch it with my toe. It's become freezing again, as fresh water has flowed over the top ledge and through the small cracks between the rocks. I feel Dragon's warm hide behind my bare back as he joins me. I don't have to ask a second time. He dips his head beneath the surface and fires the water for me. This time he stops short of boiling it. I feel the temperature with my toe.

"That's perfect, Dragon," I say, easing into the water.

I float over his semi-submerged snout for a while, and when I am clean and relaxed, I climb back up his hoard. Gold and jewels may buy soft beds, but they do not make them. Dragon opens his front claw and lets me climb into his warm grasp where I find the deepest sleep of my life.

I sleep so deeply that I don't even notice when Dragon turns into a man.

5

I awake because a jewel is jabbing me in the hip. And there is a hand cupping my breast.

I look down, just to make doubly sure that the hand is neither mine nor some small cup-shaped scale that dislodged from Dragon's claw in the night, but no. That is definitely a man's arm draped over my ribs, and a man's hand latched onto my breast.

I stiffen, and I feel a warm stomach flutter against the small of my back and a wide chest pulling in a deep breath behind me. The man sighs his breath out onto my hair, and then his body tenses. I slowly look over my shoulder.

His wide eyes are emerald green, and the hair on his head is golden, but the rest of his stunned and stunningly beautiful face is decidedly non-draconian.

He releases my breast and raises his hand, holding the appendage out in front of him as if he's never seen such a preposterous thing. He sits up, looking down at his naked and (good gracious!) magnificently sculpted body, his breathing becoming erratic.

"Dragon?" I ask.

He looks up at me, as if answering to his name. He's shaking from head to toe. I know this because I can see *all* of him. From head to toe. And he can see me, I realize. I cover what parts I can with my hands.

He makes a noise and claps a hand over his throat when he hears his own voice as if it were foreign to him. Then, he pushes himself back and away from me, slipping on treasure, and flailing in a panic.

I dive down the side of the mounded hoard for my clothes. I pull my smock over my head with unsteady hands.

I see the carpenter's satchel lying next to my kirtle and I take out Dragonbarb, just to be safe. The man's eyes *look* like Dragon's, and he had the same diamond incisor, but there's no shame in taking a few precautions. In my experience, I've found men to be the least trustworthy of all the creatures. Including dragons.

I peek back over the disrupted mountain of jewels. He's on his hands and knees and his face is so terrified and confused my heart breaks for him. I rise and take a few steps toward him, but he throws out a hand violently and makes a grunting noise that almost sounds like *stop*. I stop.

Then, he turns back into a dragon.

He's so close to me now, that I must tilt my head back sharply to see up into his eyes. He scoops me up in his claw and holds me close to his face. He makes a plaintive mewling noise.

"You're scared," I say, stating the obvious. "Have you ever turned into a man before?"

He growls, indicating the negative, but then his eyes unfocus in thought.

"You don't remember?"

He grumbles uncertainly.

"Well, do you remember anything apart from being a dragon?"

His eyes unfocus again, but he suddenly growls in frustration, and puffs smoke out his nose. Then he rears back on his hind legs, unfurls his wings, and trumpets loudly. I cower down inside Dragon's claw and cover my ears. Then he suddenly bounds out of the cave and off the side of the mountain.

It appears Dragon has had enough of this conversation.

My stomach drops as the landscape falls away. I hear the whoosh of his wings as they pound the air. He dips to the side and everything lurches dizzyingly. Trying not to be sick, I look out between his talons and see that we are circling down to his fishing lake.

As we approach the ground, he flaps his wings backward to land softly on his hind legs, and then he places me gently in the grass.

"I asked you not to take me under the water and you remembered," I say, smiling. "Thank you."

He shifts and looks out at the lake.

"Go get something to eat. It might make you feel better," I reply, interpreting his look.

Dragon nuzzles me, leaving his spicy, smoky scent on me,

and then he canters down to the lake and slips into the water. I sit down on the grass to wait.

I fold my arms over my bent knees, drop my forehead down onto them, and have a somewhat hysterical laugh. The first time I wake up with a naked man and he panics, then turns into a dragon. Although I must say, everything before the panicking part was quite nice. I don't know how old he is for a dragon, but as a man, he looked barely older than me, and I'm about twenty. Neither my father nor I knew my age when he found me, but we made a rough guess. Dragon looked young and very scared. And very handsome, of course, but that shouldn't matter. Don't know why I'm thinking on it now. This whole turning in a man business must have been some horrible mistake, and I doubt it will ever happen again.

Do I want it to happen again?

While I'm pondering this, I see the telltale V heading for me as Dragon swims just under the surface of the still lake, and then his great golden head rises from the water. He snakes across the surface silently and in moments he is onshore and dropping a load of fish in front of me.

As before, he allows me first pick. I select a decent-sized fish, gut it with a few deft strokes from Dragonbarb, lay it on a rock, and he sears it for me all before thinking of himself.

"Thank you, Dragon," I say, frowning as a thought I don't want to have starts forming in my head. "I wonder where you learned such fine manners."

He bumps me with his nose, and I reach out to rub his jaw.

"Have your fish, you magnificent lummox."

I watch him closely as we eat but he seems unflustered now, as if he's forgotten all about turning into a man. As if it were a fluke. While Dragon sunbathes, I find a few late and extremely sour berries growing around the lake. There are some edible flower bulbs that I dig up, wash, and crunch into as well. Dragon may be able to live on fish alone, but I certainly cannot.

As the day wanes, the sky darkens, and it starts to rain. I shiver violently in the downpour. Dragon scoops me up in his claw and flies me back to his mountain. He places me down gently by the side of my pool, and without me asking, heats the water for me to the perfect temperature. I feel the water with my toe, yet I don't go in the pool or take off my wet smock.

"How thoughtful of you," I say quietly. "Too thoughtful for any animal, really. Even if dragons are smarter than most."

Dragon makes a questioning noise, staring pointedly at the water as if asking me why I don't get in.

"Then there's the whole question of you not eating any of your virgins." I laugh, though it's not very funny. "You never even considered eating me. That's not very draconian of you."

He stares at me, and I have to swallow the lump in my throat to continue.

"The problem is, I think I'm beginning to understand that you aren't a dragon who accidentally turned into a man. I think you're a man who's been turned into a dragon."

He drops his long snout into the water and blows bubbles to entice me. When I still don't move, he pulls his wet snout out of the water and nudges me with it.

Why can't he just be a dragon? Tears fill my eyes, which is terribly embarrassing. I have no idea how I got attached to him so quickly, but it appears I did.

"I can't do this," I say, turning away from him.

I stride resolutely to the exit. Dragon trots along behind me, making that plaintive sound of his. I'm not going to look back, though. I really can't.

One of his wings swoops in front of me and I run into it. He catches me up and holds me as if in a hammock. Then he blows warm air on me, still thinking I'm cold. I roll out of his wing and keep heading for the exit.

"I can't stay here with you," I tell him. "It isn't right."

He clambers along behind me, every now and again nudging me with his nose and making questioning sounds.

"You are probably the most wonderful man I've ever met, but you have a very big problem in that you are currently a dragon." I leave the cave and start walking down the mountain trail.

Dragon's claw wraps around me and he lifts me off my feet.

"Dragon, put me down this instant!" I demand. His talons close around me, and I kick the inside of his claw in anger.

He trumpets loudly in response, and I must cover my ears or go deaf. He carries me back inside his cave and places me on top of his hoard.

"I'm not one of your jewels, Dragon!" I shout. "And you're not a dragon! You're a man, and you've got a terrible spell on you!"

Even saying the words make me pause in sympathy until I remember my place in all of this.

"I'm just a tinker's daughter. You need a magician or a miracle. I can fix just about anything, but I can't fix you. I'm so sorry."

I start sliding down his hoard, determined to get away from him when I hear a voice behind me. A man's voice.

"Hel-p," he groans. The word comes out forced and broken.

I spin around and see the man on his hands and knees atop his heaps of sparkling treasure.

"Help... me," he pleads desperately.

Then, he turns back into a dragon.

6

Of course, I'm going to help him. Like the fool I am.

Or try to, although I have no idea what I can do for him. I return to the hoard and sit on it. He's resting his head on his front claws, his luminous eyes staring entreatingly at me.

"I'm not making any promises, Dragon," I say sternly. "The only thing I can think to try is for us to go to Bolloxville and find out what happened. Maybe someone knows where you came from, or how you got turned into a dragon." I think for a while, tapping my teeth with my nails. "I'm going to go out on a limb and guess Asphodel had something to do with it."

Dragon growls and narrows his eyes menacingly.

"You don't remember who you are, but the name Asphodel makes you angry?" I roll my eyes. "Well, I guess that settles it. He certainly has something to do with your being like *this*." I gesture to his enormousness.

Dragon lifts his head and makes an offended sound.

"Oh, I like you very much like this," I say, laughing, "but you must admit, most people would prefer you as a person, seeing as how you as a dragon could slaughter them by the hundreds."

He grouses a little but decides an itch is more pressing than arguing with me and turns to nibble at a leg.

I go over to where I left my kirtle and start lacing myself into it. When I've finished, I look around for anything else I should take with us. The only items here other than rocks and heaps of treasure are a few more dragon scales—which I put into the satchel of carpentry tools—and the post and chains that restrained me.

I look down at the shackles and rub my wrists, remembering. I notice they don't hurt. The cuts are gone. In fact, I don't think I've felt pain in them since my bath, and even the scabs have vanished. I glance one last time at the water, wondering if it has healing properties, then I pull the satchel tightly across my body and head toward the exit. Dragon follows.

When we get outside the cave Dragon wraps a claw around me and picks me up. He holds me level with his nervous eyes.

"I'm not leaving you, Dragon. We're going together. First, you've got to fly us down to my village because there are a few things I need to settle before we go, and then we're off to find out who you are."

Dragon looks at the dark sky and mewls uncertainly.

"No," I say, shaking my head. "We can't wait until dawn. If you fly down to the village in broad daylight, you'll start a panic. And I don't want anyone to know we're leaving. It's got to be a secret," I whisper. "We," I gesture to him and I, "fly," I hold out my arms and flap them, "down," I point to the village below. "Shhh."

He makes a wise-sounding hum, and then he launches us off the side of the mountain.

I've got to get used to this. At least, I must get to the point where I don't scream bloody murder every time Dragon takes me flying. I manage to recapture my wits before we come in close enough to wake anyone with my glass-shattering shrieks, but it's still embarrassing. I've never seen myself as the screaming type.

Dragon lands us a bit outside the village, back-winging his landing so softly not even I can hear the flapping or his body alighting. He releases me into the dewy grass and stares at me. Away from his hoard, I notice that his eyes glow ever so subtly in the dark. I wonder if it helps him see better, like a cat.

"Wait here," I tell him. "I'll be back."

I start walking, and after a few paces, I notice that my right shoulder is slightly warmer than my left. I look over my right shoulder and see him shadowing me without a sound.

"No, Dragon," I whisper. "You're too big. You stay here."

He huffs smoke out of his nose in agitation.

"I can't take you to my father's house!" I whisper-shout. "You'll scare what little life he's got left out of him. Just *stay*."

I continue on, entering the town proper, and I'm nearly to the small cottage that my father and I have been renting at a very reasonable price for the past fortnight. I feel Dragon's warm body just behind and to the right of me again. I stop. I collect myself so I don't yell at him. Then I turn.

Dragon is a gorgeous naked man.

I drop into a crouch, yanking him down with me, and scan all the dark windows anxiously. Most everyone is still sleeping—I don't see any lit candles—but what if there is a new mother awake to feed a babe, or an incontinent old man relieving himself in his garden? I grab Dragon's arm and pull him behind a stone wall, forcing him to stay down.

"You can't wander into a town naked, Dragon," I hiss at him. I gesture down at his privates and immediately avert my eyes.

He puts a hand over himself and shifts uncertainly. He's trying to say something. His mouth works, and his breathing elevates.

"F. *F.*" He clenches his fists and his jaw grinds in frustration when the word won't come.

I calm myself first, for nothing would make it harder for me to speak than someone staring at me impatiently. Then I look him in the eye and put a hand on his shoulder to help him focus. I wait for him to find the word.

"Father," he says in a burst. Then he smiles and sighs at his success. He taps my chest with his fingertips. "F-father."

"Yes," I whisper, smiling. "My father. We're going to see my father."

Dragon grins like a little boy and stands excitedly. And he's still completely naked, so I avert my gaze quickly. Fortunately, as I do so, I see laundry hanging on a line just on the other side of the stone wall.

I pull him down again and hold up an imperious finger. "Stay."

I jump over the wall and snatch up a pair of breeches and a tunic, then vault back over the wall before Dragon can follow me.

"Put these on," I whisper.

Dragon looks blankly at the clothes in my hands, and I realize we could spend hours out here before he'll learn to do this. I try to keep my eyes closed as I dress him. Granted, I've already seen everything there is to see, but I draw the line at gawking at him.

Well, I gawk a little. It's just I always thought that a man would be a clumsier, rougher, and uglier version of a woman. I've always known men had different body parts, of course, but based on other women's descriptions of them I never thought I'd find those parts anything other than... unfortunate. I certainly never thought I'd find them alluring.

I help him into his tunic. I try not to touch too much of him as I pull it down over his head and chest, but he is holding my hands under his as I dress him. I suppose he's learning or maybe remembering, but every time he covers my hands with his he accidentally presses my hands against him. As I tug up his breeches and start to lace them at the front, his hands cover mine and I accidentally touch parts of him I shouldn't be touching. I jump away.

"Dragon," I say, "You should do this yourself. Just tie the laces."

I pantomime tying. He looks at me as if completely lost. He bends in half trying to see his crotch, and as he does that, pretty much everything flops out. Modesty is a lost cause, I realize. I relent and tie his laces for him.

"There. All done," I say brusquely. "Come on. Let's go."

I take his hand and pull him along behind me as we hurry over the last few parcels of property to my father's cottage. I'm still blushing furiously, of course, but I manage to pull myself together by the time we go inside.

My da is sleeping, and he sleeps like a stone. I must shake him to wake him up.

He sits up and squints at me. "Jonara? Is that you?" he asks.

"Yes, Da," I say. "It's me."

"They said you got eaten by the dragon," he says, still confused and looking put out because of it. Sometimes my Da gets confused about ordinary things and it makes him angry when he can't follow along. Like the world is playing a dirty trick on him. It happens to some people as they age, I've been told.

"He didn't eat me, as you can see," I say, making a joke out of it to ease him away from his disorientation. "He prefers fish to virgins, actually."

My da nods. "Glad to hear it." Finally, he smiles and reaches up to pull my head down to his. We touch our foreheads together as is our custom. When he pulls back his eyes are wet with tears. "I thought I'd never see you again."

"Sorry, I worried you, Da."

He gives me one last squeeze and then stands. "We'd best lit out of here right quick before the townsfolk see you and send you back up to him."

"Da—wait," I say, but he shuffles over to the wardrobe to get his clothes out, already packing.

"You're the only virgin for miles, I hear," he says. "We may have to go a bit farther than usual." He turns and startles when he sees Dragon. "Who'er you?"

I go back into the shadow that Dragon has tucked himself into and take his hand to pull him forward.

"Da, this is—" I begin but my da doesn't let me finish.

"You went and got a husband!" he exclaims.

"Oh… wait…" I stammer.

"You lucky man!" he says joyously, rushing forward with a grin and open arms to embrace Dragon. Surprisingly, Dragon smiles back and holds out his arms for a hug.

"Da," I say, trying to get his attention.

Totally ignoring me, my father reaches up and holds Dragon's muscular frame to his bent little body, thumping him repeatedly on the back.

"Our Jonara is a right smart one, my son, and as affable a partner as you could ever find. You've done yourself a good turn by marrying her. I'll be sad to let her go," he pulls back to look up at Dragon's grinning face, "though I won't be sad to have loads of grandchildren—and you look like just the one to do that trick in a jiffy," he adds with a wink. He claps me on the back. "You've landed yourself a hearty-looking husband, Jonara. Good on you!"

"He's not my husband!" I say, on my last nerve. "That's the *dragon*."

My da's spine stands straighter than I've seen it in years. "He's the dragon?" he repeats.

"Yes," I say, relieved to finally get that point settled.

"Well, then he's not a dragon, he's a Dragon *Lord*," my Da corrects like that's obvious. "Only Dragon Lords are men who become dragons at will." He nods appreciatively. "They're magical. They can do all kinds of things and they're incredibly strong. I never told you about Dragon Lords?"

"I suppose maybe you did," I reply, sighing. My Da's told me a lot of nonsense over the years. When I was little, I loved listening to him, but as I got older, I began to resent the stories that took up more of his thoughts than common sense did, and I stopped listening, just to be contrary. "But what difference does it make if he's a dragon or a Dragon Lord?" I ask.

"They're gentry, love. You're practically the wife of a king."

"I'm not his wife," I correct quickly.

Dragon wraps one hand around my hip and the other he buries in my hair in the most intimate way. "Wife," he says, drawing me toward him.

My da's eyebrows leap up into his non-existent hairline. "Well, at least I don't have to worry about you being a virgin sacrifice any more," he says, sniggering.

I disentangle myself from Dragon. "Yes, Da, you do," I say, offended, "and that's not even the issue at hand or why I came back here, all right?"

"All right, love," my da says, done with teasing me for the time being. "If you didn't marry him, why'd you bring him here?"

"Because he can't remember ever being a man and he asked me for my help. I owe him. That's all."

I ignore Dragon's hurt look. Don't know why he's hurt

about anything I said, or if he even understood anything I've said, or what any of this has to do with anything to begin with. I take a deep breath, smooth my tousled long brown hair behind my ears, and start over.

"Da. I came here because I've got to go help Dragon find out who he is and what happened to him, but I didn't want to leave without telling you I'm alive. And. I wanted to give you some money," I add, hesitating. My da hates talking about money.

"Don't you worry about that. I'm set, love," he says, waving a hand and shaking his head.

I know he's not set because he's ridiculous with money. He gives things away without charging people, saying a smile is the best payment, which it isn't when you're hungry, which we often *were* when I was too young to handle the business of things. I couldn't leave if I thought he'd go hungry again without me.

I take one of Dragon's arms, pull up his sleeve, and scratch. A small gem falls into my palm. I hand it to my father who stares from Dragon, to me, to the gem in his hand.

"That explains that flash tooth," my da mumbles, pointing to Dragon's diamond incisor.

"Don't use that gem to pay for anything," I say as I reach into my satchel. "It's too valuable and you'll draw too much attention. Use these gold coins instead." I give my father a bag of gold coins I took from the hoard.

"I can't use these, either," my da says, incredulously. "This is more than the town's worth."

"Buy the cottage and all the land around it. Say the gold

magically appeared the night I died. Payment from the dragon, or some such," I say, shaking my head as I make up the lie. "Don't let anyone know you have more. Okay? If I don't come back in a few weeks, you should leave town. You'll have plenty to remake your life. You can live like a baron."

My da chuffs sadly and looks down at the fortune in his hand. "Never wanted to be a baron. I just want some grandchildren."

He looks heartbroken, but I can't give him what he wants. Dragon is a bloody *dragon*, not a son-in-law. Da always was such a dreamer that I've always had to be the realist, whether I wanted to or not.

"I've got to go, Da," I say, noticing the lightening sky. I hurry to the hope chest at the end of my pallet and grab my road pack, already full of provisions for when we leave town. Which we always do. I add to it a fresh smock, kirtle, undergarments, and shoes. "I've got to help Dragon, and then I'll come back," I promise as I shoulder my two bags and then I take Dragon's hand again.

Da is still looking down at the sparkling gem in his hand.

"Da?" I repeat. "Did you hear me?"

"I hear you, Jonara," he says quietly. He looks at Dragon. "Take care of her," he says.

"Yes, F-father," Dragon says, bending down to give my da another hug.

"He's not *your*—" I start to explain, but I sigh and give up. "Come on, Dragon. It's almost dawn."

"Wait," my da says.

I turn and face him, trying to control my temper.

"Go to the fairies," he tells me. "They can help your Dragon Lord."

I shake my head at his nonsense. There's no such thing as fairies. "Goodbye, Da."

I pull Dragon by the hand from the cottage and into the fields of oats just beyond. I help him out of his clothes and push them into my satchel, hurrying him to turn back into a dragon before the dawn, though it is already the grey twilight of false dawn.

I suppose I'm upset. All this talk of Dragon being my husband—as if I could catch the eye of a man like him. I suppose I shouldn't be pushing Dragon to transform and fly north with the sun rapidly rising and the light blazing off his golden hide like a mirror. I suppose what we really need is for me to think up another plan, because as soon as we get airborne, Dragon is shot out of the sky.

7

Caged inside Dragon's foreclaw, I see a group of men below, clustered around a large wooden structure. I don't realize it's a crossbow until I see an arrow the size of a sapling soaring through the air toward Dragon's heart.

I scream and kick to warn him, but not in time for Dragon to get completely out of the way. He veers, and the arrow goes straight through his left wing.

Dragon trumpets and flames as he twists in the sky. I see the earth, then the sky, then a great river of fire in the air as we tumble. I am sick and dizzy as we streak across the sky like a comet, heading for the forest outside of the village. The trees are coming up fast.

"Dragon!" I scream.

He manages to re-extend his injured wing before we hit the treetops of the forest. It's enough to slow us somewhat but at great cost to him. I can hear his scream of pain, sounding somewhere between man and beast.

Branches break as we fall through them. His hind legs hit the ground and we skid. As Dragon pitches forward with me in his claw, he changes back into a man and catches me in his arms just before we both slam into the ground and then tumble some more through the leaf litter.

My ears are still ringing when I push myself up on my hands and knees, but apart from a few bumps I am uninjured. I see Dragon's naked human body sprawled and bloody on the ground not far from me. He isn't moving.

I crawl over to him, repeating his name. He's breathing, but he will not wake no matter how sharply I call out to him. He's covered in superficial cuts from the fall through the trees, but the worst injury is on the back of his left arm.

It looks as if an arrow had threaded just under the skin of his arm below the elbow and had come out again at the shoulder. But it's not two clean holes. Both the entrance and exit wounds are jagged and torn and stretched at the edges from catching the wind and stopping our fall. Blood flows freely from the ragged flesh.

I rip the bottom off my already tattered skirt and hastily tie up Dragon's arm. I have clean bandages, but I won't use them until I have a chance to clean Dragon's injury first. Right now, I just need to staunch the bleeding and get him away from here. Those hunters will be coming for him.

That enormous crossbow was made to kill dragons—it was not luck. They didn't happen upon a dragon while they oh-so-fortunately had a dragon-slaying bow on them. They must have seen Dragon flying with me over the past few days and got it ready for the next time he took to the air.

I made him fly rather than swim to go to the fishing lake.

I made him fly now, even though the sun had come up. This is all my fault.

"I'm so sorry, Dragon," I whisper.

I wipe my wet cheeks and secure my pack around the front of me. Then I get my knees under me and roll Dragon onto my back. I position him lengthwise across my shoulders and I push with my legs until I am on my feet.

One thing about being a tinker's daughter who always carried the pack? It made me as strong as a mule. I've never rejoiced in the meaty thickness of my lower body from so much squatting and lifting, but now that I find myself in this position, I wouldn't trade my round ass for anything. And though Dragon is probably the heaviest load I've ever carried, I've never been more motivated. I wouldn't say I run, burdened as I am, but I do jog along at a steady pace.

The trick to carrying a heavy pack is to keep carrying it. Get it on you so it's nice and balanced, brace your legs under you, lean forward, and just keep putting one foot in front of the other. Don't stop, especially when you start tiring.

Those hunters with the crossbow will be looking for an enormous golden dragon. Since we didn't fall straight down, but rather across the sky, I imagine it will take them a few hours to find where we landed.

When they don't find him, they might notice my tracks and decide to follow them to see if I know what happened to their prize, but they won't catch me. Not today. Bolloxville is only ten miles away, give or take. I can make out the suggestively-shaped mountain through the trees. I'll get there by dark, but only if I keep going.

"I'm sorry, Dragon," I whisper as I jog along. "I'm so sorry."

Another thing I learned being a tinker's daughter, when the road was long and the meals were few and far between, was that anyone can do anything for a day. Just one day. I can carry Dragon for a day.

He wakes twice as I plod along with him across my back. Both times he groans in confusion and pain, then falls back to sleep.

As Bolloxville nears, I am forced to put Dragon down and hide him in a hollow. I can't march into the town center carrying a naked bloody man across my back, although I wish I could. The agony of putting him down is worse than carrying him for another hour, but I manage to squat down and ease him off my shoulders and onto a thicket of ferns at the edge of town anyway.

I check his wound. It isn't bleeding any more, thankfully, and the worst of the ragged edges look clean, although inflamed. I don't think he's in immediate danger, but he desperately needs care, especially after being jostled around on my back all day. I pour water across his lips until he takes some in, sputters, and finally drinks.

"I'll be right back," I tell him. I strip off my white dress, stained red with his blood, and cover him with it as best I can. I'm thirsty, but I don't drink. We don't have enough water. I use a few precious drops to wash the most noticeable blood off my face and hands, and then I put on my darkest smock and kirtle and leave the rest with him.

"Stay down," I tell him. "Drink if you can. I'll be back for you."

As I spin away, he catches my arm. "Don't. Go," he whispers.

"I have to for a little, but I'll be back. Promise." I lean my face close to his. "I didn't lug you across that wretched forest to abandon you."

He smiles and his eyes close as his head falls back.

I leave the pack but take the carpenter satchel with the jewels in it. I can't use any of Dragon's jewels in this town, but maybe I can barter one of the better tools in the kit for a stay at the inn.

I smooth my hair as I walk toward the town center. Every ache seems to vanish as I flush with fresh purpose and doubled worry now that I'm separated from Dragon. I lick the thirst paste off my lips and teeth as I walk into the first and probably only inn in the unfortunately named village.

A woman with a bright yet empty smile greets me. "Are you eating in the tavern, or have you come to stay with us?" she asks.

"I've come to secure a room for the night, but we will also be needing supper," I tell her. Her eyes keep fluttering off to the side in distraction. "Is that going to be a problem?" I ask.

"Let me check our book and see if we have a vacancy," she says.

I follow her into the tavern to a nook at the end of the bar. She takes out a ledger and starts flipping through the pages. She goes forward to the most recently filled slot, then she pages back again, and then forward until I realize she has no idea what she's looking for.

"What did you say your name was, again?" she asks.

"I didn't," I reply haltingly.

"Oh. Of course," she winks at me like we have a secret joke between us. "And what room were you in?"

There's something very strange going on here. I glance at the barkeep. He's polishing a glass slowly and his eyes have the same far-away look as the hostess's. I glance around the room at the patrons. They sip their beers and scratch their heads as if trying to recall something. It's very quiet. If one patron begins to talk to another, they don't get far into the conversation before it peters out and they both fall back into distracted silence. I hold my hand out for the ledger.

"Let me have a look. I'll find my name," I tell her.

"Cheers," she says, smiling with relief as she hands me the book. "I can't remember whether or not I can read." Then she laughs.

I almost repeat back what she said in disbelief, but before I can, I remember what the carpenter said to his son about Bolloxville being cursed.

I notice the keys hanging in the nook. There are three pegs, and only one key left on the last peg. I shut the book with a smile.

"We'll take Room 3," I say pleasantly.

"Excellent," she replies, taking the key off the hook and handing it to me without entering anything into the ledger.

"Might I ask for a cup of water, Mistress…?" The woman stares at me blankly. "Your name," I prompt when it becomes clear that she isn't going to supply it.

"Oh, I've no name any more!" she says, laughing again, as she takes up a pitcher at the end of the bar to pour me some water. "We've all lost those here."

8

I get back to Dragon before sunset.

He lifts his head at my approach and we both smile at each other with relief. His diamond tooth sparkles in the dappled light.

"Jonara," he says.

I raise an eyebrow as I crouch down beside him. "You know my name," I say. He seems to be remembering more of his humanity the more time he spends as a human.

He nods. "Father... said."

"Right," I reply, remembering that my da used my name in front of Dragon. I frown thinking about my strange experience in town. "What's your real name?" I ask Dragon.

His eyes get that same faraway look as the people in the tavern. He shakes his head. Then, growing agitated, he tries to stand.

"Wait," I tell him. "You'll have to walk a little when we get to town. Save your strength until then."

He nods and looks down at himself as if to check for something. I notice he's put my dress over his private parts as if trying to conceal them. I look away quickly and busy myself getting his clothes from my pack. I slide his breeches up his legs, but he pulls away from me as if he's remembered to be embarrassed when I try to bring them up higher. I lean back on my heels.

"Can you... do you need help?" I ask.

Dragon tries to lift his hips up enough to slide the breeches on himself, but he cries out when he attempts to use his injured arm. He falls back, trembling.

"Here," I say gently. "Just let me. It's not like I haven't seen it already," I say, trying to strike a more lighthearted tone, yet I still avert my gaze as I dress him. "Do you need me to do the laces?" I ask, but he's already shaking his head.

He fumbles with them for a long time, but finally manages to get them secured. Somewhat. Hopefully, they'll stay up.

"Let me re-bind that," I say, pointing to his arm. I rip another strip off the rag that was my white sacrifice dress. I remove the bloody strips on his arm and look at the wound beneath. "You're starting to heal," I say, surprised, looking up from the much-improved wound to his face.

He's looking at me, not his arm. "Heal... fast," he repeats, nodding.

I drop my eyes and get back to re-wrapping him. Then, I ease him into his tunic and strap my pack across my front before crouching down next to him again.

"Ready?" I ask. He looks chagrined as I try to roll him across my shoulders.

"No," he says, refusing to be carried.

"Dragon, I can see you're healing fast, but you should let me carry you. You've lost a lot of blood and you can't walk yet."

"No," he repeats, putting his good arm over my shoulders instead. His face is close to mine as he smiles warmly at me. "You c-carry... enough."

My cheeks feel hot. He is unsettlingly beautiful. I look away and take as much of his weight as he'll allow, as I guide him slowly into town.

"Drop your head and pretend to be drunk," I tell him. He looks confused. "Keep your head down, and don't look up."

He does as I ask, and I bring him into the inn. I fake laugh and pretend to be tipsy while I hail the hostess.

"Could you send dinner up to our room? I've got to get my husband into bed before he falls asleep on his feet." I make for the stairs.

"You need help with him?" she calls after me, giving me a broad smile.

"Been handling him all day," I rejoin with a wink. "Room 3," I remind her as I tackle the stairs. "And water. We'll need extra for bathing."

I let us into our room and ease Dragon down onto the bed. My legs are quivering and threatening to give out under me. The ache between my shoulder blades has turned into a throb. All I want to do is flop down and fall asleep, but I can't. I ease the tunic up over Dragon's head again and unwrap his wound.

I find water in a pitcher. I pour some of it out into the basin.

"Drat. The water's cold," I mumble.

Dragon gives me a funny look, and then bends over the basin and breathes fire onto it.

"Oh!" I exclaim, surprised. "You can do that as a man?"

After heating the water, he gives me a bemused look. He taps his chest. "Dragon," he says.

I laugh to myself as I dip a fresh cloth into the hot water. "Yes. I've noticed," I say.

I dab at his wound, and though he grimaces and his breathing is tight, he makes no other complaint. When I'm done re-binding his wound with the clean bandages, I pour the bloody water out the window and start over with a fresh basin of water.

He heats that water as well, and then I start cleaning the rest of him. He doesn't protest this time when I undress him fully to make sure he is clean, and that there are no other wounds I may have overlooked. All his superficial cuts are gone, but he looks pale, and his eyes are falling closed by the time I'm finished.

"You need to eat," I say. "The hostess has most certainly forgotten to bring dinner."

"Rest," he says.

"Yes, I know you're tired." I pull the blanket over him. "You rest while I go down to the kitchen and see what I can get for us."

"*J-Jonara* rest," he corrects. He can barely keep his eyes open.

"Soon," I say, sighing with fatigue. "I'll be back," I say, taking too long to look at him before I leave.

I go down to the tavern to find the hostess, but she seems to have wandered off somewhere. The barkeep has his hands full, as a few more men have gathered before him. They are speaking loudly and drinking heavily.

"I'm telling you, we hit him in the heart!" a big, bearded fellow is saying.

"You hit the wing," a pox-marked man argues. "I was the only one looking up while all of you were working the gears of the crossbow. It was the wing, I tell you."

My breath catches. These are the hunters who shot Dragon. I sidle up the bar and help myself to the pitcher of water as an excuse to listen in on their conversation.

"I aimed it true," a young, dark man counters.

"You did, Glomsby, you did. Best shot in the area, you are. But the dragon veered," Pox Face replies soothingly.

"How, Crat?" the bearded man asks the pox-scarred man. "Unless he's got eyes in his feet! He was directly over us. How could he see us?"

"Dragons are crafty, Putter," Crat says wisely to the bearded man.

"Or he had help," says the fourth man in the group. He is a bit better dressed than the rest of them, and his crisp accent smacks of education, while the others have the collapsed consonants and sliding vowels of country bumpkins. "We found where he fell. Found tracks leading here. Human tracks."

The other three men stare at the rich man. "Are you saying a person picked up a dragon and carried him to town,

Barth? Is that what you're insinuate-in?" Crat asks, incredulously.

The hunters go silent as they all stop to brood on the impossibility of the scenario. Lucky for me, none of them have met my da and been regaled by one of his tales of Dragon Lords.

I put down my cup and spin away.

"Hey there. Girl," Barth, the rich man, calls.

I turn back around with a bright, empty smile on my face. "Would you like dinner? Or a room?" I ask, heading directly to the ledger nook as if I work at the inn.

Barth eyes me suspiciously. "You aren't the girl who greeted us," he says. He comes toward me. "My family has had the rent of this town for four generations, and I don't recall seeing you here on any of my visits."

I feel my heart throwing itself against my ribs. I let my eyes slide to the side like I can't quite remember.

"I thought by the way you called me—like a servant," I say uncertainly. "I'm not?" I laugh and shake my head. "I must be a patron. I should go back to my room then." I'm backing away from the bar, thinking of Dragonbarb safely and uselessly tucked inside my satchel, when the big, bearded man, Putter, steps forward.

"Leave her," he says in Barth's ear. "She doesn't know what she's about. Asphodel must have stolen her name, too."

"I don't recognize her, and that's the kind of girl I'd remember," Barth insists with a lascivious sneer. "She's not from this village."

"She could have been traveling, staying at the inn when it happened," Glomsby, the sharpshooter adds.

Barth finally relaxes. Then he decides to start taking advantage of the fact that I can't remember who I am.

"Bring us some dinner, girl. And be quick about it," he says.

I manage to grin like an idiot, though I am grinding my teeth. I have to go behind the bar to get to the kitchen, I think.

"And barkeep! Another round on you!" Barth adds as I step back into the service area.

The bartender gives me a vaguely uncertain look when he notices me in his territory, but he brushes past me and gets to his job anyway.

Barth's men grumble at his taking advantage of the people here. As I wait for the bartender to finish his pour and therefore make way for me to pass behind him, Barth replies, "They'll never remember any of this. Besides, they *should* spare us some libations as we do them a service. Dragon's bones are the only things that can kill Asphodel and break this spell he's put on them, and we're the men who are going to harvest those bones, aren't we, fellows?"

"Hear, hear," the men chant, raising their newly filled glasses.

I dart around a corner and toward the smell of food. I find a few people, including the hostess, standing in front of the bread oven, all of them drinking soup out of wooden bowls. I help myself to two bowls of the hearty chicken and vegetable soup that is simmering on the cast iron stove.

"The men at the bar want some dinner," I tell the hostess in an offhand way, and she straightens as if remembering something suddenly and hustles out to the front of the house.

I stack my bowls in one hand, tuck two loaves of freshly baked bread under my arm, grab a wedge of hard cheese, and then climb the servant's stairwell to the second floor with the pilfered dinner.

The bread and cheese I leave for our breakfast, but the bowls of soup I devour, one after the other while I watch Dragon sleep. Gold dust glitters on his skin and on the sheets, and a gem rests on the pillow next to his head, reminding me that though he is shaped like a man at the moment, he is also much more. My Da always told me that magic was an illusion, except when it wasn't. I never understood what he meant by that until now.

Maybe Dragon's bones are the only things that can kill Asphodel. But I'll be hanged if I let anyone pull them out of him.

9

I awake to what is probably the worst leg cramp I have ever had in my life.

When I reach down to rub it, I find that the pain between my shoulder blades is nearly as intolerable. Torn between two agonies, I stay where I am and groan.

I feel a warm hand touch my back. "Jonara?"

I'm sleeping on the floor next to the bed. I roll over onto my back and look up at Dragon. "I'm okay," I tell him. "Just sore."

"Did you f-fall?" he asks. I notice he still has a stutter.

I'm confused for a moment, not sure what he means by that. Then he pats the mattress.

"No, Dragon, I didn't fall out of bed," I say, sitting up. "Oh, crikey, that hurts," I moan, and I reach back and try to rub my shoulders, which doesn't really work when both your arms are heavier than rocks.

I feel his hands replace mine and begin to knead my

screaming neck and shoulders. It feels so good it takes me a few moments to realize that he's using both hands.

"Your arm," I say. I haul myself to my feet to look at his wound.

He's removed the bandage. The wound is completely healed, and all that's left is a red mark. He flexes his arm and turns it, making the muscles cord and ripple beneath the skin.

"Almost b-better," he tells me. He rolls his big shoulders. "Another d-day."

"And then you can fly?" I ask. He nods. "That's amazing," I whisper, sitting down next to him.

He's still naked, though covered by the sheets from the waist down. He notices me looking at him and moves closer, his mouth softening. I jump off the bed and hurry to the dresser and the bread and cheese I left on top of it.

"I got breakfast for us last night," I say with my back turned. "I don't know if you eat this, or if you only eat..." I feel his warmth behind me, and I turn to face him, losing my balance and nearly tipping into his arms as I do so, "...meat," I finish lamely.

"Eat bread," he says, barely nodding. He catches my wrist gently in his hand and runs his nose and lips across the inside of my arm, breathing me in. "Smell good."

"Dragon," I say, half-melting, but still tugging my hand out of his. "It's not appropriate for you to be... ah... sniffing me," I say. I try to move away from him, but his rumbling laugh and bright diamond smile make me stop and smile back at him.

"Not eat," he assures me, still chuckling and shaking his head. "Just s-smell."

He puts his hands in my hair and starts slipping it through his fingers, drawing long tresses to his mouth and rubbing them against his lips. He's still naked. It's innocent in one way, and completely not innocent in another way, and I don't know how much of this he understands yet as a man. Come to think of it, I don't know how much of this I understand, either.

I pull away from him and go to the other side of the room.

"I've decided we need some rules," I say. "Now that you are a man, you must wear clothes. We can't sleep in the same bed, and you may not touch me like *that* any more. Understood?"

He looks confused and hurt. "Wife," he says.

"No," I say, holding up a hand. I point to myself. "Dinner."

He gives me a disbelieving look. Then he comes toward me, his eyes heavy and his smile slow. "White d-dress. Mine."

"Yes. I was your sacrifice," I explain, edging back until I hit the wall. "Not your bride."

He stops, and his face falls. "*You* s-say husband."

I pause in thought and then remember. "Oh. Last night? Yes, well, I had to tell the hostess you were my husband, or it would be improper if we shared a room. But you're not really my husband."

He looks like I struck him. He shifts on his feet uncertainly. "You c-carry me."

"I carried you because you were injured," I say. "I'd never abandon you, Dragon."

He takes the last few steps toward me, smiling gently. He places two fingers on my collarbone. "That is wife," he says.

I could just let this happen. Let him believe whatever he wants, but I know this must stop. He isn't mine. He isn't even *his* yet. All of this is a dream. It's like one of my father's romantic tales of magic, danger, and love, and I can't let it continue because when it's over I'll be the one left out in the cold. My father's stories made for great distractions, but they never put a roof over my head. I push Dragon's hand away.

"You don't know who you are," I say sharply. "My father said you were a lord. Men like you don't marry tinker's daughters. For all you know, you already have a wife and family who are desperate for you to come back to them."

I step around him and cross to the bread and cheese, though I have no interest in eating it any more. My hands are shaking because I've finally given voice to a fear that I've harbored since I woke and found him in human form. My fear is that while I stare at Dragon with stars in my eyes, there might be other people who are waiting frantically for this man to come home to them.

I know what it is to be left behind. I waited for my parents. They never came back for me. My Da happened upon me and took me as his own, but what if Dragon has left a little girl of his own, and no one as kindhearted as my Da comes along for her?

"I'll help you because I'm your friend, Dragon, but that's all," I say. "When we find out who you are, we must go our separate ways."

When I turn back around, he's sitting on the bed. He's covered himself with the blanket.

"Sorry," he says, his voice husky. He taps his chest, looking for the words. "I was w-wrong." He forces a smile. "I s-see now."

"Good," I reply, but it doesn't feel good. In fact, it feels horrible. I smile cheerfully anyway. "I'll try to find us fresh food and water, and I'll be right back. You stay here. Okay?"

"Okay," he replies, nodding. He looks at me. "You go. I stay."

I throw myself out of the room and stand against the closed door. I lean my head against it for a moment, trying to steady my breath. The door starts to feel warm.

I pull my head away and turn to run my hand over the wood. I let my hand rest there for a moment, feeling it continue to warm as if another, hotter hand was on the other side, mirroring mine. I can hear Dragon on the other side of the door and I smile, even though I shouldn't. I'm finding it very hard to stay upset with him. That's a problem that will only hurt me in the end.

I turn away and go downstairs to a bustling business at the tavern this morning. From what I can gather in a quick glance, the hunters are making quite a show of how they have shot down a dragon, and many of the befuddled townspeople have wandered in to watch. Finding themselves in a tavern, the townspeople are now ordering food and drink as if they have no other jobs to do, or as if they have forgotten those jobs, is more likely.

"It won't be long now, chaps!" Crat, the pox-marked hunter, says from a tabletop as he waves an early morning beer over the heads of the childlike townspeople. "We shot that dragon in the *wing*, we did."

The townspeople gasp and clap.

"That Drake won't be flying anywhere, though he's hidden himself. Crafty things, dragons," Crat continues after taking another pull off his ale. "But we'll find ole' Forked Tongue, and when we do, we'll take his bones and kill Asphodel with 'em!"

A great cheer goes up. My stomach drops as I think of these people dancing around Dragon's dead body.

Barth marks me as I stand there, watching. I adopt the vague smile I see on others' faces and drift about as if I have no set place to be, although I make sure to waft in the general direction of the ledger in the nook.

I pour myself a cup of water and idly flip the ledger open, looking for any information on the stables. If the excitement in this inn is any indication, this group of hunters won't be the only ones out for Dragon, and we need to get away from here as quickly as possible. Even if Dragon were healed by tomorrow, we still couldn't fly with half the countryside aiming to shoot him in his soft underbelly. We must either walk or ride, and I'd much prefer to ride. If we skirt the Forest of Woe it might dissuade anyone from following us, but we will need mounts to do so carefully. I would not like to encounter a troll, or worse, just outside that wretched haven for monsters without a fast horse beneath me.

As I'd hoped, the inn does have a small stable of horses for hire in case one of their patrons finds themselves without a mount. The stall numbers for the spare horses conveniently match the room numbers. One, two, and three. I shut the ledger and put it back in the nook. When I turn, I find Barth standing uncomfortably close to me.

"What would a patron be doing, looking in the books?" he asks me, moving still nearer.

"Am I a patron?" I ask vaguely. "Oh, yes. Of course, I am. I keep wondering about my horse."

"Your horse?" Bath asks disbelievingly. "You've forgotten nearly everything else, yet you remember that you have a horse?"

"Well, I'm sure I must have a horse," I say, guffawing to hide my shaking voice. "I didn't walk here."

"Didn't you?" he asks. "My tracker, Putter, saw some unusual footprints in the forest, right around where the dragon fell."

"Dragon?" I ask. "Oh, yes! You've downed a dragon. How brave of you."

He lifts one side of his mouth in a smirk, wondering if he heard a faint note of mockery in my tone. "Putter said that a small footprint, probably a woman's, was pushed into the earth as if she weighed many times what a normal woman would weigh."

I look askance and swallow. "I should probably go in search of my husband," I say, but Barth wraps a hand around my upper arm.

"She would either be very fat," Barth continues, squeezing my arm muscles in his hand. "Or very strong. Strong enough to carry a heavy load." He runs his hand up my arm. I can smell the beer on his breath, and I turn my face away. "You're a sturdy one, aren't you?" he murmurs.

"Let go," Dragon says sharply.

Barth's eyes dart behind me and he blanches, releasing my arm. Dragon puts me behind him and keeps advancing on Barth. Dragon is not only taller, wider, and thicker than the reedy, paunchy, and slope-shouldered Barth, but there is also something menacing about the way Dragon looks at him. He's never looked at me like that, certainly, and for the first time, I see in Dragon a devourer of men.

"I was... um... telling your wife... that... ah. Oh, dear," Barth stammers as he cowers before an angry Dragon.

"Don't touch," Dragon says to him.

"My apologies," Barth squeaks, like a mouse under Dragon's boot.

I rush forward and put myself between them, facing Dragon. "A misunderstanding, my love," I say, running my hands across Dragon's chest.

Dragon pulls his gimlet stare away from Barth and looks down at me, startled by my intimate gesture.

"Our horse is ready," I tell him, pressing myself against him to break him from his forward-leaning stance. His hands come up to cup my shoulders tenderly.

"W-worried," he whispers.

"Me too," I admit quietly.

At this point, all the hunters have become aware of the altercation between their master and the big, blond man, and they've come to cluster behind Barth. Dragon looks up from me and gets that predatory gleam in his eyes again, surrounded as he is by men who hunt him. I turn and lean my back against Dragon, trying to push him away, but the stubborn beast seems bent on fighting.

"We've been trying to leave for days, it seems. Or maybe

we haven't. I can't remember," I say laughingly. I thump myself against Dragon's chest. He doesn't budge, the lunkhead. "If I could but find the hostess to settle our bill, we could go—oh! There she is."

I grab Dragon's hand and pull him toward the back of the house, though I've seen no one. When I glance back, I see Putter whispering in Barth's ear.

"We've got to leave here, now," I tell Dragon, leading him to the servant's stairway. "Go back to our room and get our bags. Meet me in the stables around back. Do you have any itches, perchance?"

Dragon tilts his head curiously, then nods, smiling. He reaches into his pocket and pulls out a handful of gold coins. "Already s-scratched," he says.

"I'll pay the hostess. Go," I tell him when he hesitates to leave me. I shoo him up the stairs and start gathering up provisions. I don't know where we're going just yet, but I'll figure it out when we are well away from here.

The hostess catches me loading food into a burlap sack. Her first instinct seems to be to tell me to stop, but she pauses long enough for me to pour Dragon's gold into her hand.

"Payment for room, board, and horse," I tell her, closing my hand firmly over hers. "Keep it hidden... and forget we were here," I add, though I don't think I need to. She stares at me, astonished, while I go out the service door to the stables.

I see that stall three has a nice-looking pony in it. Nothing fancy, but he seems young and well cared for. While I'm checking to make sure our mount is properly shod and not about to go lame, the pony begins to prance. I release his foot and back out of the stall.

Suddenly, all the horses begin to throw their heads or kick at their walls, as Dragon enters the stable. The horses whine and try to sidle away from him.

I realize what's going on and sigh. "They're scared of you, aren't they?" I ask Dragon.

He nods regretfully.

"Why would they be scared of you?" Bath asks as he and the rest of the hunters emerge from their hiding places around the barn, surrounding us. "Could it be because you smell like a dragon?"

10

Crat has a crossbow aimed at Dragon's chest. Putter and Barth each have their swords drawn. Glomsby, the sharpshooter, is in the hayloft with another crossbow trained on Dragon.

Dragon angles himself in front of me and drops the bags. His eyes drift around the room, taking in every man and his position.

"Where are you hiding it?" Barth asks. "We know you took our dragon somehow. Tell us where he is, and you and your wife can go."

Dragon looks back at Barth, who draws away from him fearfully.

"D-dragon here," Dragon says, tapping his chest.

He rolls his shoulders and I see his tunic strain to reach across his shoulders and back, as if his body is growing and thickening under his clothes. His fingers stretch into talons and when his lips part I see the gleaming tips of fangs. When

Dragon takes his draconian form, he does so in an instant. This evolution into something not quite man and only part dragon is something I've never seen before.

Neither have the hunters, from what I gather, because they seem to shrivel away from him in awe and terror as if they can't believe their eyes. The horses are bucking and kicking in a panic now as the spicy, smoky scent of Dragon grows stronger.

"He's a bloody Dragon Lord," Putter groans in dismay as if only now he's realized his error.

"Shoot him!" Barth cries over the sound of the hysterical horses.

I hear the twang and hiss of a crossbow being fired, but Dragon has already moved out of the way. He's moved over me, I realize, as he rolls me down onto the hay-covered floor.

I see the bolt from the other crossbow skitter uselessly across Dragon's impenetrable back. With both bolts fired, and time needed before Glomsby and Crat can reload, the hunters are practically helpless against Dragon.

He rolls off me holding two knives that are the length of his forearms, though I have no idea from where he conjured them, and he faces off against his attackers. Putter rushes him like a bull, but Dragon deflects his sword easily, and with a deft twist of his wrists disarms the big man. He lands a kick and sends Putter sprawling into a hay bale.

I dive for the satchel at this point and pull out Dragonbarb. Before Putter can rise, I crouch beside him and hold the knife to his throat.

"Stay down," I tell the tracker.

Now that Putter has been contained, Barth decides that

it's time for him to fight or be forever shamed. Dragon doesn't even raise his blades to Barth. As he dodges the clumsy thrust of a desperate man, Dragon spins a knife in his palm to face the blade backward, punches Barth in the face, and knocks him senseless with one blow.

Dragon glances up at Glomsby, who had reloaded. Rather than throw a blade, Dragon walks up to Crat, pulls the unloaded crossbow out of Crat's petrified hands, and throws the crossbow at Glomsby just as he is firing a second bolt, ruining the shot. Then Dragon grabs Crat and puts the edge of one of his blades to his throat.

"Down," Dragon calls to Glomsby. His talons and fangs have retreated, but his clothes still strain against his added girth. I see spots of blood on his wrists, but I didn't catch how he was injured.

Glomsby looks down on Dragon holding Crat and wavers for a moment. Dragon meets the dark man's eyes. Then he suddenly lets go of Crat, spins the knives in his hands so that the blades point out again, brings his arms together, and the blades seem to disappear up opposite sleeves.

After a moment of deliberation, Glomsby announces, "I'm coming down now."

He's got another bolt loaded into his crossbow, but he shoulders his weapon to climb down the ladder. As he does, Dragon looks at me and waves me over.

I reluctantly release Putter. I'm shrugging at Dragon, not understanding why he would want to let both of our hostages go. When I get to him, Dragon tucks me behind him.

"C-closer," he snarls at me.

"I'm practically in your back pocket," I reply incredulously.

"Closer," he demands, smoke puffing out his nose.

"Fine," I whisper, pressing myself against this back. "But it's rather hard to see with a big hulking dragon in your way, you know."

I hear Dragon rumble, as Glomsby comes to stand in front of him, his crossbow still shouldered, and his arms across his chest. Putter stands at his right and Crat manages to shuffle to Glomsby's left, though he is less staunch of heart than his mates and hangs back a little.

Glomsby and Putter share a look. "What's the matter with his speech?" Glomsby asks me, gesturing to Dragon. "Is he foreign?"

"He forgot he was a man until just the other day," I reply.

"Coo. That's a bad case of it, all right," Crat says sympathetically. "Only those in the north have had their names stolen for so long they've forgotten they're human."

"What do you mean?" I ask, trying to come out from behind Dragon, but he keeps stepping in my way. "I'm perfectly safe, you big, daft dragon," I say, finally getting out from behind him. "What happened up north?" I remember that Dragon supposedly flew down from the north.

"That's where Asphodel comes from, right?" Crat answers.

"Once Asphodel's got your name, you forget who you are and what you do. Eventually, you forget you're human," Putter says, his tone hushed. "Up north, where Asphodel first started stealing names, there are towns where everyone's been nameless for so long, they don't even act like people any more."

"Asphodel is coming south, and he'll keep coming until someone stops him," Glomsby continues. He turns to Dragon. "You're a Dragon Lord. You're one of the only things that's supposed to be able to kill him. Asphodel's got an army now, but I'd join *your* army if you went against him."

I shake my head. "He barely remembers how to speak, and you want him to gather an army?" I ask, incredulous. "He's still more dragon than man—I only got him to start wearing clothes a few hours ago."

"We have no king. We need a leader," Glomsby argues. "Soldiers would follow a Dragon Lord."

"It's all about the banner, really," Putter says musingly. "It's got to look inspiring."

Glomsby turns to him. "What are you talking about banners for?" he asks.

"I'm just mentioning that a Dragon Lord would have a nice banner," Putter says, shrugging his big shoulders sheepishly. He continues even when he probably shouldn't. "No one would follow a farmer into battle. I mean, who wants to fight under a banner with a big vegetable on it?"

"It's not about the *banner,*" Glomsby snaps, put-upon. "Soldiers would follow the Dragon Lord because he can actually *kill* Asphodel, while normal people with normal weapons just *can't* because of some spell or the other. And he's a bloody great fighter. He disarmed all of us in under a minute and no one even got hurt except for that idiot Barth, but he deserved it. That's someone I want in front of me in a battle, what about you?"

"Well, yeah," Putter concedes. "He's ruddy terrifying is what he is. Send him out first in a battle and everyone would scatter."

"Good squires," I interject at this point because I simply can't stand it any longer. "Before Dragon can do anything, he must get his name back. He needs to know who he is. He might have a family."

"I had family," Glomsby retorts angrily.

"Me too," Putter adds quietly. "In the north."

"North, south, won't matter soon," Crat says, grimacing. "If you've got family anywhere, I expect Asphodel is going to get them."

Dragon turns to me with pleading eyes. "Kill Asphodel," he says quietly so only I may hear. He touches his chest and gets that far-off look again. "My q-quest?" he says, then growls in frustration. He stammers more when he's upset, I've noticed. "Can't r-remember. Help m-me, Jonara."

For one moment I wonder what would happen if I said no, but as soon as I think it, I know I could never say it to him.

"Of course, I'll help you, Dragon. But...," I continue, stopping him before he gets too excited, "you can't face Asphodel again until you find out why you failed the first time."

"How do you know he failed?" Putter asks.

"Because he hasn't got a name," Glomsby replies like it's obvious. Putter still looks confused, so Glomsby continues explaining. "That means he must have faced Asphodel before, and Asphodel took his name, right?"

"Right."

"That means the Dragon Lord lost!"

"Oh," Putter groans, finally getting it. "Right. Yeah, you best get that straightened out beforehand. Wouldn't want to go making the same mistake twice, would you?"

"No. He wouldn't," I say.

"Also, where are we going to get an army?" Putter interjects, scratching his beard.

How did these men ever manage to pull themselves together long enough to shoot Dragon down? Putter may be a good tracker, but Glomsby seems to be the only one who has a level head on his shoulders.

"Having a common cause helps," I explain, "but what's actually required to raise an army are people who need jobs and someone who can pay them lots of money."

"I haven't had a regular job in years," Crat says, guffawing. "That's why I took this one, even though it's ruddy dangerous." He looks nervously at Dragon. "You don't hold grudges, do you?"

Dragon cracks a smile and shakes his head.

"Good," Crat says, sighing. "That's a relief."

"I know plenty of men who yearn to go to war against Asphodel, and not just for a job," Glomsby says.

"Could you get word to them?" I ask.

"Certainly. But most of them have no weapons or provisions. The only reason Putter and I brought Barth along was because he had enough money to build a proper dragon bow."

"I can get the money," I promise.

"How?" Glomsby asks.

"I know a guy," I reply evasively. "Now. Do we leave

Barth out here while we continue discussing our plans, or bring him inside?"

Dragon carries Barth into the tavern, and we take a table. While Barth's comrades revive him and explain the situation, I go back into the kitchen and see what I can do about breakfast for all of us. Someone at the inn still has enough sense to make bread and stew, although those seem to be the only things on the menu. I find what's left of the butter and cheese in the larder and coax the hostess into bringing us a meal.

This village is running out of food, and every day the people in it lose more of their ability to care for themselves. They need help, but I don't know how to give it to them. Still chewing my lower lip, I quit the kitchen to rejoin the table.

I turn the corner to find Dragon's eyes seeking me. He breaks into a glowing smile and pulls me close to him when I take the seat beside him.

Barth is sitting as far away from Dragon as possible, brooding. I shelve that worry for now and deal with Glomsby, who is eager to confer with me and Dragon. He leans across the table, his dark eyes burning.

"Asphodel's power grows with every recruit to his army. We must raise an army to meet him," Glomsby says.

"An army?" I say, turning to Dragon, speechless.

"Men will follow Lord Dragon," Putter says with a nod in his direction.

"But an army requires more than men," I argue. "It requires weapons, provisions, and..." I trail off, stymied.

What does an army require? The same thing all risky endeavors require at the onset, I suppose. "Money."

"M-money I have," Dragon says quietly to me.

I narrow my eyes at him and lean closer. "Are you sure you want this?" I ask him.

"Yes," he whispers, his eyes pleading with me.

I look at Glomsby. His eyes are just like Dragon's. They're all looking to me to help them start a war, and in truth, I know that someone must stand up to Asphodel. They intend to do the standing and it appears they've decided that I've got to do the planning. I haven't much of a choice.

Well, then. How would one go about mustering an army and preparing for war? I suppose it would be akin to readying a tinker's pack before a long journey, only multiplied by about a thousand. Multiplication I can do. And for the first time, I'll be able to do it with a very large purse that is filled with as much gold coin as I can lay eyes on.

"Money, we have," I tell Glomsby, including Dragon. "Willing fighters *you* have." Glomsby nods sharply in agreement, and I continue. "What we need is to get our money safely to your people who will use it to procure weapons and provisions to fight Asphodel."

"What money?" Barth asks derisively.

"What's your plan, Lady Jonara?" Putter asks, ignoring Barth.

I've never been mistaken for a Lady before, and I'm about to correct Putter when Barth makes a snorting noise.

"She's no Lady," he scoffs.

Before he can continue, Dragon grabs him by the front of his tunic, lifts him over the table with one arm like he's made of nothing but paper and twine, and pushes him forcibly onto his knees in front of me. Dragon's incisors have grown into fangs again, and the diamond one glints when he speaks.

"*Lady* Jonara," Dragon growls down on the prostate Barth.

"My apologies, Lord," Barth squeaks, covering his head with his arms. "She is the Lady Jonara. That's clear to me now."

Dragon hauls Barth up to his feet and steps away from him. "Leave now," Dragon commands.

"Thank you, Lord," Barth replies quickly, and he runs out the front door.

Dragon takes my hand and sits, pulling me down into the chair next to him. "Please. P-plan," he says, encouraging me to continue, though in truth I never stopped. It's amazing how quickly one's mind can organize itself when one has no worry of cost. But all that money needs to be kept safe. Safe but accessible. Someplace these fighters Glomsby promises can get at the money they need to arm themselves against Asphodel.

"I need ten trustworthy people, iron, and a forge," I announce.

"Done," Glomsby says, nodding his head. "May I ask for what?"

"If we're going to start a war, we're going to need a bank."

11

The first thing I must secure is a working forge.

Glomsby leads me across the town center to a brick building that lies close to the river, but downstream from the townspeople. There is no smoke coming from the double-sized chimney, and when we get inside, I see my fears confirmed. The forge fire has gone out.

"There's plenty of coal, but we need time to get it hot," I tell them. I start sorting through the sheet metal and rods that the blacksmith had on hand.

Dragon tilts his head into the kiln and breathes blue fire until the coals turn white. When he pulls his head out again, he's got soot on his cheek.

"Hot now," he tells me quietly.

I take a rag and wipe the soot off his cheek. "Honestly, Dragon," I say, "Every time I turn around, I've got to give you another bath."

"My baths b-better. Bubbles," he says.

"Yes, your bubbles are much nicer than a rag," I admit, laughing. When I turn back around, everyone is staring at us.

"He just breathed fire," Crat says, blanching.

"D-dragon," he says, haltingly pointing to his chest.

I suppress a grin.

"Now," I say, clearing some room on a wooden work-table, "taking into consideration the state of this forge, I'd say the blacksmith in Bolloxville is no longer an option for the work I need done. I could do it all myself, but that will take too much time."

I take a sheet of paper and a charcoal nub off a shelf full of sketching materials and lay the paper out.

"You're a blacksmith?" Putter asks hesitantly.

"Tinker's daughter," I say. "My specialty is this." I draw the rough plans for a warded lock.

"Mazes?" Putter guesses.

"Locks," Glomsby corrects, his eyes wide. "You can make strongboxes? With locks and keys?"

I nod. "The work will go faster if I have someone else heating and hammering for me while I file and shape the pieces. There's a blacksmith in the village beneath Dragon's Mountain." They look puzzled. I roll my eyes and get it over with. "It's called Taintsville," I admit reluctantly.

"Are you from Taintsville or Bolloxville, milady?" Putter asks.

"She's a tinker's daughter. She t'aint from here, and she t'aint from there," Crat says, his face spasming with poorly repressed laughter.

Whoever named the villages in this area was either drunk

or had a terrible sense of humor. I let them get it all out before continuing.

"The blacksmith's name is Lakonius. Give him this." I hand Putter three gold coins. "Prepayment for his work. If he brings his carpenter friend, the one with a young son, the carpenter may have this." I hand Putter two gold coins.

Putter stares down at the riches in his hand. And then back up at me.

"Ride out with spare horses now and you should return by tomorrow," I say.

"Yes, Lady Jonara," Putter replies, bowing before he sweeps out of the forge.

Odd, that. Being bowed to.

"And what shall I do? Give me a task," Glomsby begs.

"You must get word to those willing soldiers you promised me," I tell Glomsby. "I need three days to get the lockboxes ready. In that time, I expect you to bring me ten trustworthy people, and tenfold men to serve as their guards. Can you do that?"

"Yes, milady, and I'll do one better. I'll get you an army," Glomsby promises, bowing before he leaves me. This bowing thing is starting to become a habit. I'm not going to say I hate it.

While I never intended to organize a war, I may as well do it right, from top to bottom. "Crat," I say, stopping him before he can slink out.

"Yes—ah—milady?" he replies.

"Find Barth," I say, twisting the nib of charcoal between my fingers. "If he's had a change of heart where our Dragon

Lord is concerned, bring him back to us. If not, find out what he's planning to do against him."

"So, spying, milady?" he asks uncertainly.

"Exactly."

Crat gives me a lopsided grin. "Now *that* I can do," he says, dipping his head—not quite a bow, but good enough—before sauntering out of the forge.

"Dragon," I say, standing up and facing him. "Would you like to learn how to make a warded lock?"

"Yes," he says, nodding.

I must wrap my face and hands while the rods heat, but Dragon is fireproof, and therefore better served by stripping down. I make him keep his breeches on, though I'm sure he'd prefer to be stark naked. He hasn't gotten completely used to clothes yet. I turn away from him while he takes off his tunic and do my best not to stare at his bare chest.

I teach him how to turn the metal in the fire. How to hold the hammer. How to strike the glowing metal evenly. How and when to quench the metal in a barrel of cold water to build its strength.

He takes to smithing quickly, telling me in his brief way that working with metals feels natural to him. I suppose for someone who can breathe fire and create gold beneath his skin that's to be expected, but even I am surprised by how even and precise his work is. And how lovely. Dragon sweats gold dust. Not enough soft gold is falling into the metal to weaken it, but I'm noticing that Dragon's work sparkles with tiny flecks of light.

"I'll always be able to spot one of our locks," I tell him as

I inspect another sheet of metal that he's hammered out for me.

"Good," he says. "You will remember m-me."

I tip my head, bemused. "Like I could ever forget you, Dragon."

"I've forgotten me," he says. Then he turns back to his work. The clang of his hammer makes it impossible for me to promise anything else that I don't know if I'll be able to keep.

We work all day without stopping. By evening, I have ten designs for ten different warded locks and diagrams of the exact shape and size needed for every piece inside them. I feel Dragon peering over my shoulder as I re-check my drawings with calipers.

"How does it w-work?" he asks me.

"The key goes in the hole," I say, pointing to the drawing. "These notches in the key line up with these metal plates inside the lock that stops any key but the exact one from turning. Only by turning a key all the way around can you slide back the bolt that holds the lid of the coffer closed."

He stares at the drawings until he finally smiles and nods. "Used locks. Never understood how l-lock work."

I smile back at him. "I've always liked figuring out how things worked." I look down at my drawings. "It makes me feel… I don't know. Safer, I guess."

I feel Dragon lean closer to me and I look up at him. He is striped with soot and gold dust, and he smells like spice and ashes. His green eyes, though smaller in human form, have not changed in how they regard me. For a moment I almost expect him to nudge me with his snout as if he were still that enormous beast listening patiently to me while I spill out my heart atop his hoard.

He looks away and steps back. "I'm hungry," he says. "Need food."

I realize I'm practically throwing myself at him. I straighten up and smooth my skirts. "I can check the inn for food, but..."

"No," Dragon says, shaking his head. "They forget. I m-must... feed them."

I nod. "Okay. This was bothering me too. How am I going to get supplies into town for these people over the next few days?" I start to think out loud. "After we establish a bank, trade will follow, and we'll allot a stipend, but until then—wait. Where are you going?"

Dragon has turned and walked away from me. He leaves the forge through the back door and crosses the large courtyard between the forge and the river where we draw the water for the quenches. He sits down at the riverbank to take off his boots.

"Not *you* feed, Jonara," he says, exasperated. "Me feed. I. I f-feed them." He stands and takes a deep breath, searching for the words and how to say them.

It's hard. I want to speak for him. I want to jump in and guess what he'd say, but I calm myself and wait for him to speak for himself. But he decides against it.

"Turn around," he finally says, smiling to himself and shaking his head.

I do as he asks, though I don't understand why. When I hear movement, I look over my shoulder. He's unlacing his breeches and pulling them off. I turn back around hastily.

But I peek.

He changes into his draconian form, going from man to dragon in an instant, and I'm still staring. Man, dragon, he is an awesome beast no matter what form he takes, and I will not deprive myself the pleasure of looking at him.

Dragon slides himself silently into the cold rushing waters of the river. I go to the riverbank and watch for his flashing hide under the surface. He's gone for a while. When he comes out of the water, he waits on the riverbank with his front claw outstretched for me.

"You want me to climb up?" I ask. He nods once, and I climb up, wrapping my legs around his long neck.

His scales seem to shift under me, repositioning themselves until I have more stability in my seat. I even find that he has flared a scale where each of my feet come to rest against him, and I drop my heels and hook my feet under them. Locked in, I ride him easily as he walks to the town center.

The lowering sun is glinting off him brazenly, and it seems that every window we pass has a staring face framed inside of it. When Dragon gets to the town center, he opens his mouth and dozens upon dozens of fish spill out. Then, he trumpets loudly to alert anyone who might have missed him. People begin to gather cautiously. From my seat atop Dragon, I wave people forward.

"A gift from the Dragon Lord!" I call out. "If you are hungry, come forward and take a fish."

The people are silent and still for many moments. They stare at Dragon in awe, but eventually, hunger wins out over fear, and a few brave individuals snatch up a fish and run away with it. When this occurs without incident, more step forward. A scrum is just about to erupt, when Dragon growls and huffs smoke through his nose, making the people dive back in fear.

"Take only what you need," I tell them. "The Dragon Lord will provide more when you need it."

When Dragon is satisfied that the people are gathering up the fish in an orderly way, he goes back to the river. I climb down from his neck when he holds up a claw for me, and again he disappears into the water. This time he resurfaces quickly, and when he opens his jaws, five medium-sized fish spill out at my feet.

He picks up his breeches with his front claw and nudges me with his snout.

"What?" I ask as he pushes. He grumbles and waves the breeches in his claw. "You want me to turn around, so you can change? I guess I did make that rule, didn't I," I say as I turn away from him.

"No peeking this t-time," he says behind me, back in his human form.

"You saw that, did you?" I laugh, embarrassed. "Sorry."

"Get basket... for fish," he replies, chuckling.

I go inside and find a basket to carry the fish, and Dragon and I take them to the inn. We give the basket to the hostess to make a fish stew for all the inn folk. Then we sit down in the tavern to wait for our meal. I look at my hands, blackened with charcoal.

"I need to bathe," I say.

"I stay here," Dragon replies. He's looking down at the table and not at me.

I stand but pause before leaving. I don't know why I feel like there's something unsaid between us; I just know there is. He finally looks up at me.

"I will wait," he says, the words heavier than they should be.

I hurry upstairs and find only cold water in our room. I suppose I could go back down and ask Dragon to warm it for me, but I don't. I take a cold bath and wash my hair. I'm shivering by the time I'm done. I braid my wet hair, put on a clean smock and kirtle from my pack, and return to the tavern where Dragon is waiting.

When he sees me, he breaks into the same relieved smile he seems to always give me when I've been out of his sight for any amount of time. When I sit, he takes my hand and pulls me closer to him.

"Cold," he says, feeling my fingers in his.

"I miss bathing with you," I say before I realize how that sounds.

He smiles, his diamond tooth glinting. "Me too."

My cheeks get hot, thinking of our warm baths together. He was a dragon then, but I wonder how different the man and the dragon are.

"How much do you remember about those first few days in your cave?" I ask.

"Seeing you. In chains," he says slowly. "Call me b-beautiful. First thing I... remember. Like being... born."

I don't know what to say. He hasn't answered my question, exactly, but I'm too shaken by what he said to press further.

The hostess comes with the fish stew and I lean back,

suddenly aware of how close to him I've drawn. We eat our stew in silence and then climb the stairs to our room together. As we get to the door, Dragon stops.

"Let me sleep... in there?" he asks.

"That's not—," I begin, shaking my head.

He holds up a hand, stopping me. "I won't," he breaks off and takes a breath, looking for what to say. "Husband you?" he tries, as if asking me if he got the right word.

I laugh because his expression is funny and because I'm nervous. He takes a breath wanting to say more. I wait.

"Every time you g-go, I think... I'll be a dragon." He shakes his head as if to say that wasn't what he meant.

"Is that why you're always so relieved when I come back?" I ask. "You think you'll turn into a dragon without me?"

He makes a *not quite* face and tries again. "Town people," he says, waving a hand toward the stairs, "they f-forget more and more."

"The longer their names are gone, the more they forget being human," I say, and then I realize what he's trying to tell me. "But you're *remembering* more about being human."

He nods and smiles. "Being a dragon... easy. Happy forgetting." Dragon touches his temple, his face pained, as if to show troubled thoughts. "Being a man... hard. R-remembering hard."

I nod in understanding.

"Worst after sleeping. I w-want to be a dragon. To forget." He looks down like he's ashamed of this, then he looks up at me and smiles. "When I see you... I want to be man. I want to-to remember... you. So I fight."

I'm an idiot. A simpering fool who shouldn't be allowed near sharp objects or lit fires because only the most lame-brained lunkhead would unlock the door and let him follow them inside. Which is precisely what I do.

12

Dragon is as good as his word.

He does not try to "husband" me. Which, after removing his tunic and my kirtle, and lying down with him pressed against my back for a full hour of sleeplessness on both our parts, becomes absolutely intolerable. I know he's not sleeping. He knows I'm not sleeping. We're both lying here, so awake to each other's touch it's as if the darkness itself starts to throb around us, holding in a stifled scream. Yet, he keeps his word, insufferable beast that he is, and eventually, I fall asleep.

As I wake, I pull myself tighter to the solid warmth I cling to. I wrap my leg more firmly around my anchor, burying my face closer to its beating heart. I smell spice and smoke and the salty sweetness of skin.

"Jonara," Dragon sighs, waking.

I feel his hand curl around the back of my neck at the base of my skull. The pleasing pressure rouses me enough that I become aware of how I am sprawled across him like a shipwrecked sailor.

I open my eyes and see the swelling of his bare chest. I run my hand over him and see gold dust puff up and sparkle above his skin in the honeyed light of sunrise. I look up at his face to find it tilted down so he can look at me.

"Beautiful," I say.

"Yes," he agrees. "You are."

I laugh silently against him. He rolls over on top of me, laughing as well, and buries his face against my chest as he holds me under him. It's the most natural thing in the world to wrap my arms and legs around him. Like a cup catching water. He pushes himself up onto his forearms and looks down at me, startled and hopeful.

There's a knock at our door, saving me from myself.

"Forgive me, Lord Dragon," says Putter haltingly. "Lady Jonara, I have the blacksmith and carpenter you bade me fetch. They await an audience with you in the tavern."

"Thank you, Squire Putter," I call out. "We'll be down shortly."

The moment is gone, and I remember myself. I try to release Dragon, but he holds himself over me. He's trying to say something, so I wait.

"I would... wouldn't," he stammers and stops. I feel his body bunch up with frustration. "I would not... take you." He shakes his head. "Advantage. T-take advantage of you. Never," he says passionately.

"I know," I reply.

He tilts his head down to kiss me. I put my hand on his

shoulder before his lips touch mine. I sit up and push him back.

It hurts to look at him, so I get up and find my kirtle instead. "If anyone is taking advantage, it's me. You don't know any better. It's dishonorable of me to allow things to happen between us that might... trap you."

"But, you're not," he says, shaking his head.

"Not intentionally, but you could be trapped all the same," I say, tying my kirtle fiercely rather than meet his eyes. "And since I'm the only one with more than five days of life experience, I have to do the right thing for both of us. I'm a tinker's daughter and you're a Dragon Lord. Get dressed."

I need to get away from him. I tuck Dragonbarb into my belt, find my boots, and carry them outside the room to put them on. While I wait for him, I re-braid my hair. As soon as Dragon appears fully dressed, I turn and start toward the tavern. He catches my arm and makes me stop and face him.

"I can't... say e-everything I want," he says haltingly. It's harder for him to talk when he feels misunderstood. "But I'm not... child."

His face bright red, and his throat as tight as a coil, Dragon brushes past me and goes downstairs. I take a moment, just long enough to convince myself not to cry, and then I follow Dragon downstairs and into the tavern where Lakonius, the carpenter, and the carpenter's son are waiting with Putter.

As soon as Lakonius sees me, his shoulders drop. "What's all this about, Jonara? You were supposed to be...," he laments.

"The Dragon Lord doesn't eat people," I reply, glancing

back at Dragon. "Although, he might make an exception if you anger him."

Lakonius stares ashen faced at Dragon. "That's not—" he says and stops.

"The dragon? Yes, he is," I reply. "Lord Dragon, this is Lakonius. He's a fine blacksmith. And this is the carpenter—what's your name?"

The carpenter stares at Dragon until I snap my fingers at him to bring him around. "Ellison," he answers, startled into speaking. I gesture to his son. "That's my boy, Jack," he answers, still staring.

"Are you really a dragon?" Jack asks excitedly.

Dragon huffs smoke out his nose and smiles broadly so the boy can watch as his incisors grow into fangs.

"Amazing," Jack sighs, utterly transfixed. "A real Dragon Lord. Da. This is the *best* job you've ever brought me on!"

"Let's hope it's not your last," Ellison replies wearily.

"Can I be your squire?" Jack begs Dragon, practically jumping out of his seat. Dragon smiles at the boy's enthusiasm. "Or a page? I'm not greedy, I'll start as a page and work my way up!"

"Now, now," Lakonius cautions. "Let's see what Jonara—"

"*Lady* Jonara," Putter corrects hastily, pulling a face. His eyes dart over to Dragon, probably remembering how Dragon dealt with Barth when he scoffed at that honorific.

"Er—*Lady* Jonara," Lakonius amends dubiously, "has got planned for us first, Jack."

"If you'll follow me to the forge," I say, but Dragon touches my arm.

"Hungry," he says quietly to me. "Eat first. Then forge."

Lakonius stares fearfully at Dragon. "Please, milady. Let him eat first."

I see the hostess wandering around aimlessly, and I wave at her to come over. She looks confused like she doesn't know why a stranger would be hailing her.

"I think she's forgotten she works here," I say under my breath.

Dragon nods and leans close to speak to me privately. "Go. Tell her... she's hostess," he advises. "She wants... someone... t-to tell her... who she is."

I look up at him. "Is that how it was for you?"

"You talk to me." He rolls his eyes. "Never *stop* talking." His smile grows sad as I laugh at his teasing. "You talk like I was a man. I wanted... t-to talk back. I became man."

He's still hurt, and a little angry with me, but neither of us can avoid this feeling of sharing something important and personal between us.

"Excuse me, milord. But are we *ever* going to eat?" Jack asks.

I shake myself and look over at the four sets of eyes staring at me and Dragon. "Yes, we're going to eat, Master Jack," I reply. Then I narrow my eyes at him. "Just keep your fingers away from Dragon's mouth while we do, or he might snap one of them up."

As I stride purposefully toward the hostess, I hear Jack saying, "I wouldn't mind if a *Dragon Lord* ate one of my fingers. It'd be a good story."

I tell the hostess who she is, and then I direct her to bring us some food. After a moment or two of haziness, she comes out of her fog and responds with purpose.

"There was an order of fish delivered last night," she says crisply. "I'll have some bread on your table presently, and would you care for tea or ale?"

"Tea, please," I respond, "and what shall I call you?"

Her eyes grow hazy. "Don't know," she replies, her fingers idly stroking the cover of the ledger. I notice that she always seems to go back to it and open it like she'd written in it a thousand times. She said she didn't know how to read, but I believe she's just forgotten.

I look over at Dragon and an idea occurs to me. "Would your name be in that book?" I ask.

She looks intrigued. "Maybe?"

I open the ledger and start at the beginning, reading the first few pages that log the establishment of this inn. I feel Dragon's heat on my shoulder as he joins me.

"This is the Waverly House, run by Mistress Iofe Waverly," I read. I look up at her and see recognition sneaking across her face.

"Mistress Waverly," I say commandingly. Her eyes meet mine immediately, and I smile. "You are Mistress Waverly!" I say.

She gives me a bemused smile. "I am." Light dawns across her face. "I am Iofe Waverly." She reaches out and clasps my hand in hers, squeezing it tightly. "Mistress Waverly," she whispers. Tears fill her eyes. She looks around her as if newly returned from a long journey.

"Good morrow, Mistress Waverly," I say, glancing at Dragon, who is watching me keenly. "I am Jonara."

"Milady," she says, tears flowing freely down her face. She pauses to wipe her eyes and nose on her smock and then she straightens herself with dignity. "Your order will be ready in a trice. Please make yourselves easy, milord and milady. I'll see to your needs."

"My thanks, Mistress Waverly," I say.

"Him?" Dragon says, pointing at the vague-looking bartender. "His name?"

Mistress Waverly looks over at the barkeep, and though she starts to say something, no words come out.

"I should know it. He's worked here for years," she says, flustered. "I can remember his birthday, but not his name, isn't that odd?"

I frown and look down at the ledger. I open it and find a page that records the libations inventory, and the person who took that inventory. While I'm looking at the page, I can read his name, but as soon as I lift my eyes, the name slips my mind. Stolen.

I walk over to the bartender and read from the ledger. "Limond," I say. "You are Limond, the barkeep."

When I look up his face is as bright as day. "I am!" he exclaims. "I am Limond. Thank you, milady!"

I give Mistress Waverly the ledger. "You must not take your eyes from the page while you read out the name, or it will slip from your thoughts, but once you give a name back it will stay fixed, I think. I don't know how many names in this book fit with the people in this town, but between this, marriage licenses, and deeds for land in the town hall, I believe you'll be able to give back much of what's been stolen."

She looks down at the ledger in her hands. She gives a crisp nod. "I will do just that, Lady Jonara, starting with my cook." Mistress Waverly strides purposefully into the kitchen.

"How did you... know?" Dragon asks.

"I didn't, really, but my Da told me once that the largest part of magic was illusion. It's all in your head," I reply. "Asphodel can steal names out of everyone's heads, but he can't change what's been written down on paper."

Dragon is looking at me with a small smile. "Your father... w-warned me you were smart. Should have l-listened."

I narrow my eyes and smirk at him. Cheeky Dragon. "He also told me that anything stolen can be restored," I add.

"Hope so," Dragon says, the glint in his eyes going out. He touches his chest. "Stolen," he whispers.

I put my hand on his arm to make his eyes meet mine. "You're going to get your name back. I promise you."

He shakes his head like I've misunderstood him again. "Wasn't talking... about n-name," he says heavily.

I trail behind him as we return to the table. Sometimes I think I understood him better as a dragon.

❧ 13 ❧

While we break our fast together, Putter quickly explains to Lakonius and Ellison what Asphodel had done to the people here in Bolloxville, and in many more towns to the north.

"Bloody Asphodel," Lakonius curses, banging a fist on the table. "He could do this to any town—to our town—and what if we've no one clever like you, Jonara?"

"Lady Jonara," Putter reminds him swiftly, his head tilting slightly toward Dragon.

"Er—Lady Jonara," Lakonius amends awkwardly. "What if no one comes along and gives us back our names?"

"It's true," Putter says. "Asphodel will go on doing this until there's no one left who remembers they can read."

Ellison shakes his head, his worried eyes on Jack. "He can't get away with this."

"He won't," I say.

"How are we going to stop him?" Ellison asks. "Begging your pardon, but apart from the Dragon Lord, we're just a handful of working men and women. How are we going to go against Asphodel?"

He strikes me as a sensible man, not used to getting involved unless he must. It's men like Ellison we'll need to convince to defeat Asphodel.

"Will you follow me to the forge?" I ask.

Putter begs off. After riding straight through the night, he must sleep a few hours. The rest of us cross the town square, and on our way, we pass by the bartender who is herding small groups of people into the inn and right to Mistress Waverly and her ledger.

"She'll name them all t-today," Dragon says softly enough that only I hear him.

"Yes, she's quite industrious," I note. "And I'd wager that as in innkeeper, she knows every farmer in the area and how to get supplies around."

"Yes," he says, smiling softly at me. "But, I meant... other towns... up north. N-need this kind of help."

"You're right, Dragon. I didn't think of that," I say, a bit embarrassed I hadn't.

"Need people w-who read. N-not easy," he reminds me quietly.

There's no reason for him to keep his voice down. Now that I think of it, he usually only speaks to me, and if he does say something loud enough for others to hear, he keeps his speech to a word a two. I can guess that he is embarrassed by his stammer, but he shouldn't be. I feel a flare of anger in my breast, but before I can address this with him, we arrive at the forge.

"Lakonius. Ellison. Young Jack," I say, smiling at the eager look on the boy's face, "you will begin by building these." I show them the designs for the lock boxes.

"You drew these?" Lakonius asks.

"It's how we've made a living, my da and me," I reply.

"Oh, this is a lovely complication," Ellison says delightedly.

"Never been able to devise my own warded lock," Lakonius admits. "Can't quite work out how you get the second prong to pass around if the first is—oh, I see how you did it. Helps that you drew all these little bits and bobs like you were holding them real close up to your eye."

"Now, nothing will make them completely impenetrable, but the Lord Dragon has supplied something that will make a good go of it. I want you to line the lockboxes with these," I say, taking the dragon scales from off the shelf.

Ellison greedily takes them from me and runs his hands over one. "I don't think I can cut this," he says.

"You won't need to," Lakonius answers, taking a dragon scale of his own and training his eye on it. "You make a wooden frame, we'll lay the dragon scales over it and then hammer metal plates atop that."

"Oh, that could work, that could work," Ellison mumbles excitedly. "Yes. These will certainly slow anyone down. Would take days of smashing to get through. But for Asphodel locks aren't enough. Is it true hard dragon scales like this are spell-proof?" he asks Dragon.

Dragon nods once in reply.

"And we'll bring you more," I promise.

Lakonius and Ellison continue to pore over my drawings and the dragon scales, and as they do so, I sheepishly bring Ellison his satchel.

"Here now, I thought I'd lost that," Ellison says when he recognizes it.

"Not lost. Just rented for a time," I reply.

He eyes me. "I suppose you'll be wanting those gold coins back?"

"Keep coins," Dragon says loud enough for all to hear. Everyone freezes. They stare at him, waiting for him to say more, but he looks over at me, his eyes widening, and his jaw clamping shut.

"What the Dragon Lord has given you is yours to keep. Though it may seem like a fortune to us, to him it is of little consequence," I say, speaking for him, though it pains me he feels embarrassed about his stutter. "It is his coin we will be putting into these lockboxes and sending out to pay for an army. His coin will also help make *these*."

I pull out my sketch of all the different weapons needed to outfit an army. Alongside the sketch of each piece of armory, be it a sword, a spear tip, or an arrowhead, I've written down how many I think we'll need. The silence stretches a bit long.

"They're just rough estimates, really, but somewhere to start," I say as if that pardons the large numbers I've jotted down.

"Piss up a rope," Ellison whispers. Jack laughs, and his father looks sharply at him. "Don't you repeat that, now."

"Aw, Da," Jack moans.

"This is probably half the steel in all the land," Lakonius says, scratching his head.

"Finding enough of the raw materials could be an issue, although it wasn't here," I say, gesturing to the rods and sheet metal on hand in this very forge. "And it might just take every scrap of metal in every forge across the entirety of the land, but the Dragon Lord has the will of the people on his side, and the wealth to see their will enacted."

I feel doubt creeping in, now that they see the hard numbers and I look at Ellison. "You were right when you said that we can't let Asphodel get away with this, but wrong when you assumed that simple working men and women couldn't stop him."

I stand up tall and look at each of them in turn. "We have the means, and we have a champion. We, the simple men and women of this land, have the most to lose, and *we* are going to gather an army, confront Asphodel in battle, and then the Dragon Lord will defeat him in single combat!"

In the following silence, I realize that I had been projecting that last bit of my oration rather passionately. They're all staring at me, quite taken aback, and with good cause considering my volume. I smooth my skirts and nod my head to let them know I'm all done ranting for the moment. My gaze lands on Lakonius who is staring at me, gob-smacked.

"Does your father know how terrifying you are?" he asks.

"Call m-*me* dragon," Dragon comments, head lowered. He's laughing quietly at my expense, but I'm just so happy he's decided to speak so others can hear that I laugh along with everyone else. I divide up the plans for the lockboxes and give Lakonius and Ellison a chance to look them over a bit more. As they study my drawings, Dragon catches my hand and pulls me aside.

"Must get... hoard tonight," he whispers. "As man... c-can't make enough."

"You make more riches when you're a dragon," I say, smiling. "I'd noticed that, actually. You don't need me to scratch you as much."

Dragon looks at me longingly. "Different... itch."

I take a breath to say something, but words fail me. It's surprising how often that happens with him.

"We'll need to get this forge a bit hotter," Lakonius calls out, breaking us apart.

Dragon goes to the forge, bends his face to the embers, and breathes blue flame on the coals. The room swells with heat. He gestures to Lakonius to shovel some more coal into the forge, and though awed by Dragon, Lakonius hurries forward to comply.

"These boxes will be forged with dragon fire, they will," Lakonius says proudly.

Once the artisans are back in their element and given clear plans, they know what to do. Lakonius heats metal in flame on one side of the room, Ellison lays planks and begins to hammer the framework of a metal coffer together on the other, while Jack shuttles between the two of them, assisting them both.

Dragon and I leave to return to the inn, but before we depart, I watch Jack as he takes two separate sets of orders at once. The boy runs between the two men, juggling tasks, skipping between the embers and the sawdust, all the while keeping the jobs separate. And I can't believe I never saw it before.

I gasp and look at Dragon. He raises his eyebrows knowingly at me, but puts a finger up to his lips, gesturing for me not to speak yet.

As we walk across town to the inn, I ask Dragon, "How long have you known Jack was a girl?"

Dragon grins and shrugs. "Whole time." He touches his nose. "Smell difference."

I shake my head at him, speechless.

"They hide g-girl." Dragon frowns, looking deeply troubled. "Not get eaten...by m-me, probably."

"Why didn't you tell me?"

We get to the inn and he stops us outside, his breathing ragged and his throat working. I wait for him to be ready to speak.

"S-she's like... you. Hidden... because she's... a g-girl."

I look at him askance. "I'm not hidden, Dragon."

He nods emphatically. "Hidden... behind man... y-your whole life." He struggles, fighting to say every word clearly. "You... more than j-just... someone's daughter. You say... you are Tinker's daughter... and I am Dragon Lord... we can't be... together. But Dragon Lord... tinker's daughter... are only n-names we have... that don't matter. Not to me."

He goes inside, but I need a moment. I sit down on the stoop and watch the townspeople. Some are coming out of the inn, newly restored to themselves, and others are going in, blank and nameless.

I don't know whether I'm one of those coming or going any more.

When I finally enter, I see Dragon leaning against the bar, waiting for me. His brooding look breaks as soon as he sees me, and though he doesn't smile, he brightens. And of course, I stand there, staring at him for far too long, before I realize my own foolishness and signal for him to join me at Mistress Waverly's ledger nook.

"Lady Jonara, Lord Dragon," she says fondly. "How may I help you?"

"We were wondering," I pause and share a look with Dragon, "how you would go about feeding an army."

Mistress Waverly is not the type of woman to go around looking shocked, and even in this instance, she manages only a brief, "Oh dear," before she nods crisply. "Well, you'll need ample funding," she begins, ticking it off on her finger.

"Which we have," I say.

"And connections with farmers, drovers, wheelwrights, and warehouse owners—which *I* have," she says, and then looks between us. "So it's true? You're going up against Asphodel?"

"Yes. And I will kill him," Dragon says, without a stutter.

"But Asphodel has an army," I add. "Which we need to confront for the Dragon Lord to get to him. We have the money, and the soldiers are on their way. Now we just have to feed them."

Mistress Waverly breaks into a wide grin. "No one has ever gone hungry at the Waverly Inn," she says. "Though I'd happily watch Asphodel starve on my doorstep." She calls over her shoulder. "Limond, I'll be in my office for an hour or so."

"Right, then," Limond replies from the bar.

"Follow me," Mistress Waverly says, snapping the ledger shut and tucking it under her arm. "We'll get some numbers down in the book, and I can start making orders."

It takes us much more than an hour. Money is no object, but the rest is a little harder to figure out. Mistress Waverly takes the lead here, and neither I nor Dragon have any objection to that. We end up having our lunch in her office. I take a quick break to bring my list of needed arms to Putter and send him out to start enlisting the help of all the neighboring forges. When I return to Mistress Waverly, we sketch out a rough plan that includes aid to the towns up north, and finally, I stand and shake the woman's hand.

"Tomorrow morning you'll be getting a lockbox, filled with coin, which you may use at your discretion," I promise.

She shakes my hand, briskly, then her eyes fall. "He made me forget my husband, you know," she says. "Gone these last five years, but not to me. Not until Asphodel..." She looks between me and Dragon, sits, and takes up her quill again. "Give me your full names to write down. That way if Asphodel steals them, I can give you back to each other. The only thing worse than losing someone you love is forgetting them."

Dragon's face darkens, but his eyes flicker with a thought. He's looking at me accusingly. "Name gone," he says, and then he quits the room.

"Thank you, Mistress. I will return on the morrow," I say, quashing her attempt to apologize, as I chase after Dragon.

I see his golden head glinting above the crowd that has formed in the tavern. Many people impatiently await Mistress

Waverly to reclaim their names, and I lose Dragon in the disorderly jostle.

I run out into the street. I look up and down the main thoroughfare. Then I rush to the forge and look in. I run back to the inn and search over the tavern again. I go back out onto the street, but I can't find him. He's gone.

14

"Dragon!" I scream.

When I don't get an immediate answer, I scream his name again. He's left me. That look in Mistress Waverly's office. He's remembered something about his past and left me. Has to be. People stop and stare. They point and whisper my name. I hear a sound like a wet sheet being shook out, a few startled shouts, and I turn in time to see Dragon alighting behind me.

His chest is bare, and great red-gold wings arc from his back. Apart from the wings he is in human form, but his wrists are bloody, and he holds two long daggers in each hand. He strides toward me, fangs extended and knives ready.

People near us run away from his ferocious aspect, but I sob with relief. I throw myself against his chest and wrap my arms around his neck.

"You ran off!" I yell into his throat.

His wings wrap around us, hiding us from view, and he

holds me carefully against him, trying not to cut either of us on his two blades.

"Went back... to the room," he stammers quietly. "Get hoard tonight. Must r-rest first."

"No, Dragon," I say, pulling back as far as his sheltering wings will let me. I wipe my face and look up at him. "You didn't leave Mistress Waverly's office because you wanted to rest. You left because of what she said about loved ones."

He nods and looks down. "Her story... reminds you... about me... m-maybe having... another w-wife." He swallows the lump in his throat. "She's wrong."

"You don't know that," I say, sighing.

"I do."

"How?" I ask.

"Her heart... was empty without... h-husband memory. Mine is full of you."

I drop my head against his chest. The stubborn monster. He just doesn't get it. "What am I going to do with you?"

With my forehead leaning against his chest, I notice his bloody wrists again. I take his wrists in my hands, keeping the knives pointed away from me, and look up at him.

"What's this? Why are you bleeding?" I ask.

He nods. "My bones," he says. Then Dragon sheathes the blades under the skin of his forearms.

I lurch forward as soon as I see him piercing his wrists with the blades, trying to stop him, but even as I move, I see the blades sink in and the skin sealing back together behind them. I grab one of his wrists in my hands, swipe the blood aside with my thumb, and see the perfect skin underneath.

"There isn't even a mark," I whisper.

Dragon shakes his head, his wrists passive in my grasp.

"Does it hurt?"

He considers. "A little." He rolls his eyes and smiles. "Pulling my b-bones out."

"I suppose that would hurt," I agree. "Your bones are blades?"

He frowns in thought. "Sometimes." He almost says more but shakes his head again instead. "Back inside now."

Dragon's wings release me and curl back, disappearing into the skin of his shoulders and arms and leaving no trace. I see now that we're surrounded by a staring crowd. They're relieved, but confused when they see that there is no emergency, which makes me feel embarrassed for screaming.

I grimace up at Dragon as we walk together into the inn. "I guess I overreacted," I say.

"Why?" he asks. "Only gone... m-moment."

I look down at my feet rather than at the stares that follow us up the stairway to our room.

"My Da found me when I was six," I finally say. "I was young, but old enough to remember my real parents."

"What happened t-to them?" he asks, opening the door to our room.

"I don't know. They left one day and never came back. I waited for weeks. I had no food. I slept in the street." I swallow, surprised at how quickly the tears come at the thought of this. "I never knew what I'd done wrong," I say, wiping my cheeks.

Dragon sighs, looking dismayed, standing in front of me. Letting me cry. "I won't... leave you."

I know he believes that. He believes it so deeply, I'm starting to believe it. I shiver at a draft coming in the window.

"Why is that open?" I ask him.

"I jumped... out," Dragon replies as he crosses to close it. "Heard you scream."

I think for a moment. "Can you fly to your mountain as I saw you—a man with dragon wings?"

Dragon nods. "But can't carry you." He shifts from foot to foot. "Lie down. I'll s-sleep on... floor."

"I'll never be able to fall asleep," I say.

"Try. Long night."

I begin to untie my kirtle, and he turns his back to me and goes to the washbasin. He rinses the blood off his wrists while I get under the covers. He goes to lie down on the floor, but I stop him.

"Will you sleep next to me?" I ask, still feeling shaken. He nods and joins me in bed, wrapping his arms tightly around me.

"I won't... leave you," he repeats quietly into my hair.

It's such a strange feeling to fall asleep when it's still light out and wake just after sunset. I feel heavy and sluggish as I pull myself out of bed, and follow Dragon down to the tavern. We eat a quick supper, which revives me somewhat, and then we stop at the forge to see how they've fared.

Putter has joined the artisans at the forge, and I find him hauling coal in leather sacks for Lakonius. He tells me that he has sent word for every working forge to begin firing arms, but there was little need.

"Half the countryside has already armed itself," he informs me. "They all know Asphodel is coming. The problem isn't steel, it's food. Farmers can't grow and fight at the same time."

"Leave that to me," I reply with a curt nod of my head. "Mistress Waverly and I are making plans."

Putter shares a look with Ellison. "She's even scarier than he is," he says, nodding toward Dragon.

"You should hear her give speeches," Ellison agrees. "You won't know whether to pick up a sword or shit yourself." He points a quick finger at Jack. "Don't you go repeating that, now."

I wave off their good-natured teasing and have a look at their progress. The frames for all ten lockboxes are done, but they still need to be sheeted with metal. The locks themselves are far from finished, although the rough pieces have all been struck.

"Great work," I say, though I wish they were further along. "Unfortunately, I must ask you to keep at it. We need at least one finished box by tomorrow morning."

"Aye," Lakonius agrees without complaint, though he is pouring sweat. "We'll get one done before we knock off if you need it, milady."

"We do," I reply. "Because when Lord Dragon and I return in the morning, we will be filling it with gold."

"All right, then," Ellison says with a nod. He pulls himself up and goes back to his workbench. I see Jack slumped over on the drafting table, resting. I follow Ellison and speak privately with him.

"Does Lakonius know?" I ask, nodding at Jack. Ellison freezes for a moment, unwilling to talk until he's certain he's been caught. "Dragon and I both know Jack is a girl," I tell him. "But does anyone else?"

"No," he says, sighing heavily. "We came to Taintsville not six months ago, and I didn't want my only child eaten when she got a few years older. But it wasn't just about the dragon. Jack is handy, right skilled she is, and she loves it." He scratches his head. "I wanted her to do what she loves. She can't do it as a woman."

"I did," I argue.

Ellison shakes his head. "How many towns have you and father had to leave in the middle of the night? Did he ever explain why?"

I draw back from him, remembering nights my father came to me saying that we'd outstayed our welcome and no more.

Ellison continues, "Your name was the only one in the lottery, and it's not because no man likes the look of you. The world hates a clever woman. I don't know why it must be so, but there it is."

I watch Jack startle awake when the sound of Lakonius's hammer rings out again. She jumps up and immediately finds herself a job to do.

"And how much longer will the world hate us if all we are taught to do is run or hide?" I ask Ellison. "Jack should be allowed to be whatever she chooses—girl or boy—and if Lakonius won't teach her to smith when he finds out, I will. She will be safe with me."

"Jonara," Dragon calls. I nod at him to let him know I'm coming, and he slips out the back door.

"Thank you," Ellison says, though I can tell he's still troubled.

I squeeze his arm. "Don't worry. Jack is strong," I say. "She will find her way."

Ellison smiles at me warmly. "I hope so, milady."

I join Dragon outside by the piles of crates. He's already shaking out discarded and empty leather sacks that once held coal. I search through the heaps for some rope that might be large enough to reach around Dragon's neck.

"This one might do," I say, after holding it up and passing it through my hands several times.

Dragon eyes it and gives me an uncertain look. "Not long enough."

"Then we'll have to tie a few together and make do," I say.

"I can carry you... h-here," he says, holding up his hand to demonstrate claws.

"No," I argue. "You'll be carrying sacks of gold."

Dragon shakes his head. "Tie... g-gold to my neck."

"And what if a rope breaks and a sack of gold falls? People would be combing the woods for ages. Bandits would abound. It would be chaos."

He looks at me like I'm crazy. "W-what if y-*you*... fall?"

"I won't," I assure him, grinning. "Your neck is quite secure. I've ridden it twice now and it's better than a saddle. It'll be like riding a horse."

"Fat horse," Dragon grumbles, reminding me of what I said when I first sat astride him. "Fat f-flying horse," he amends, building on the joke and making me laugh in earnest at the image his words conjure. Yet, after only a few moments, Dragon grows serious again. He catches my shoulders in his hands. "Wind. Very fast."

"I know," I reply, looking up at him. "But I've got strong legs. Remember, I carried you across a forest."

He runs his hands down my arms. "Turn around," he relents, his voice unsteady.

I do as he asks and hear him stripping off his clothes. I tilt my head, not really spinning it all the way around, but threatening to do so.

"N-no peeking," he chides.

We both laugh at our game, and when I turn around in earnest it's to see him changed into his draconian form.

I walk up to his big head and raise my hand. "Hello, Dragon," I say.

He drops his snout and lets me rub him along his jawline. I love the smell of him, and his spicy perfume is so much stronger when he's a dragon. I want it all over me.

"That's a thing of beauty, that is," Lakonius says from the doorway.

I jump back, although I don't know why. I suppose I wasn't expecting an audience, but now that they're here, I ask for help. I gather up the sacks and Dragon's clothes and climb up onto his neck. Lakonius and Putter use the rope to tie my legs down, and when I feel secure, I signal to Dragon.

He leaps into the air, his wings pounding downward in powerful strokes. I am flattened against his neck by the force of it, yet after the initial press, I find I can sit up and look around. There isn't much to see in the darkness—just stars and the moon—but it's glorious. The air is exceptionally cold, and I make a mental note to dress more warmly the next time.

Thankfully, the flight is short. It doesn't take more than a few minutes and we are landing on top of the mountain in front of Dragon's cave.

I dismount and turn my back to allow him privacy to change into his human form, but he nudges me with his nose toward the entrance of the cave. After a few bumps I understand his meaning, and I go down into the cave with him following me in his draconian form.

We stand and stare at his hoard. I notice that not all his gold coins are the same size. I lift a few and turn them over, weighing them in my fingers.

"Is this coin half of this one?" I ask him, holding up examples of each.

He nods. I search around at the bottom of the pile for even smaller coins that have sifted beneath the bigger ones.

"And this? Is it a fraction of that one?" I ask, showing him others.

When he nods again, I make up my mind.

"Although the gems are more valuable, they are harder to regulate. Each gem's value will alter depending on its size, color, and cut," I say. "The coins also have different values, but this works in our favor, for the smaller ones can be used to make up the value of the larger. I think to set a standard, we should use the gold, and we should only take what will fit in the ten lockboxes."

Dragon makes a huffing noise.

"I know it seems like such a waste, but after traveling my

whole life I've learned that nothing is more important to peaceful trade than having a standard value for money."

He finally nods his head. He brushes a large gem with one of his talons, making a questioning noise.

"I think we should push the coins we don't use, and all the gems, into the lake," I say, cringing.

Dragon grumbles.

"The gold and gems will be hidden there, and the water will do them no harm. If we ever need them, only you could swim down far enough in one breath to retrieve them." I shrug at him. "I'm sorry, Dragon, but wealth isn't just having a lot of something. Wealth is having a lot of something that's rare."

He slides his luminous green eyes over to me and hums in his throat. Though he uses no words, I can hear his approval. Before we start our work, Dragon gives himself a good scratch. Then he rolls over in an avalanche of gold and jewels. His big body makes the cave boom as he throws himself down on his back. Then he looks at me and makes a plaintive sound.

"All right, you silly beast," I say, grinning. "I'll scratch your belly."

I spend some time getting under every bubbling scale. He purrs and hums as I crawl from his belly to his back, down his tail, and up to his face, taking pleasure in the feel of his smooth hide under my hands. I even get around the branching crown of gold and horn around his head. I empty his hide of every spare bit of treasure he's been building up over the past few days. When I get the very last gem and coin out from under his chin I smile up into his eyes, pleased with myself for the job I did, and he turns back into a man.

My hand is on his cheek. He presses my hand more firmly against him.

"Jonara," he whispers, stepping toward me, and lowering his mouth to kiss mine.

I turn my back on him hastily and step away. "I did not mean to… I wasn't trying to…" I'm too flustered to form a complete sentence.

"I thought, the way you t-touch me…" he says, trailing off.

I glance down at my hands, covered in gold dust and heavy with his enveloping scent, while he pulls on his breeches behind me. "Yes. Well. You were a dragon," I say, feeling guilty.

"I'm always Dragon," he snaps, like it should be obvious.

"But it's different when you're—" I wave my arms wide to indicate him larger. "Isn't it?"

"A little," he admits.

I hear him laughing under his breath. "Jonara, the mousie."

A snort escapes me, and I turn to face him. "I look like a mouse to you?"

He smiles secretly, looking down, and I feel such a tugging in my chest that I decide I don't want him to say any more. I don't want to feel anything more for him. I take a resolute step away from him before he can find the words to answer me.

"We'd better get started or we'll never be done before

dawn, and then we'll have to go through the blasted water to get out of here, and I don't want to drown again this week," I say, snatching up a leather sack.

He comes around in front of me and snatches my sack out of my hands. "Yes. We sh-should start," he says, annoyed with me for not letting him finish. He walks away and starts filling *my* sack.

I stand there, sputtering for a moment. When I see his shoulders shaking with laughter, I realize that he's teasing me. Trying to get me to react to him. I needn't dignify his silly behavior with a confrontation. I go and get my own sack, muttering "impossible stubborn monster" to myself.

We fill the sacks with shed dragon scales and gold coin. Gold is heavy, even just a small measure of it, but Dragon is immensely strong, even in his human form. While I can barely drag the sacks when they are but a tenth full, Dragon easily hoists two full sacks in one hand. It isn't long before we've divided tasks. I sort while he moves and carries. Luckily there are more scales layered in with the treasure and I believe we will have more than enough for our lockboxes.

We're done relatively quickly. When the sacks are full, Dragon turns back into his draconian form and uses his big body to shove most of his hoard into the deep side of the lake a section at a time. When he's done, he turns back into a man and helps me push in the smaller mounds. We stay silent as we watch empires of wealth sink beneath the black, secret waters of the mountain.

When we're nearly finished, and I've seen nearly every shade of jewel imaginable but one, I ask him, "Why are there no diamonds? I know you *can* make diamonds because of your tooth."

He doesn't answer me right away. "Diamond is hardest." Something about his tone makes me turn and look at him. "Diamond is pain." He touches his chest. "In here."

"Heartbreak," I say softly. "So, your heart's been broken, then?"

Dragon frowns. "Don't remember."

"Then, how do you know?"

Dragon looks impishly at me. He spins his hand, and a coin appears like he's performing a magic trick, though we both know it's no illusion.

"Gold is soft. I make it... when I'm... happy," he says, smiling. "That's why... so much gold dust... when I'm with you."

I can't help but smile as he chafes his hands together quickly and sends gold dust puffing around us in a cloud like he's still a magician doing tricks for me.

His eyes suddenly round with sadness and he twists his head on his neck. A look of deep pain crosses his face as he reaches a hand back to scratch between his shoulder blades. He holds his hand out to me and releases a blood-red ruby into my palm.

"Hard. Hurts."

I look at the crystallized drop of blood in my palm.

He taps his diamond tooth. "Hardest," he says. "Can't make it... without... t-terrible pain." His hand drops down to touch his chest again. "Broken heart... is the w-worst pain, no?"

I nod and go to the edge of the lake. I open my hand and let the jewel sink under the dark water.

"We won't trade in your pain," I say. "Gold will be the coin of the realm from this day forward."

15

I ride on Dragon's back while he carries the sacks of gold in his talons.

We return to the forge well before dawn. Though he's so large he barely fits into the courtyard behind the forge and looms well over the roof of it when seated, Dragon backwings so quietly that he barely makes a sound or disturbs more than a few fallen leaves. He drops the gold. Then he tries to lie down on top of it, which is utterly ridiculous.

"What are you doing?" I ask. "You're too big. You'll never fit on the top."

Dragon grumbles and turns around like I've seen cats do when they're looking for a way to get comfortable. When he's finally settled for resting just his chin and part of his long neck on top of his gold, he holds out a claw. I climb on and he lowers me to the ground. I put his clothes down for him and turn away to enter the forge so that he might change privately.

I go in through the back door and find two lockboxes finished, another three nearly so, and Putter, Jack, Lakonius, and Limond—the barkeep at Mistress Waverly's inn—all soot-darkened and scattered about on various pieces of furniture as if sleep had overcome them mid-task.

I go to the drafting table where Jack is slumped over my drawings. From my hiding place on the shelf behind her, I take down my final drawing and wake her.

I put a finger over my lips to indicate that she should be quiet as soon as she opens her eyes.

She sits up and looks around, but makes no sound.

I pick up a piece of charcoal and a spare bit of paper and write— *can you read?*

She frowns seriously, her lips moving as she silently sounds out every letter. It takes her a few moments, but I see her light up, look at me, and nod eagerly when she makes out the words.

I smile at her, then I lay the final page of my designs in front of her.

When a set of warded locks is struck by one artisan, they are different enough that the key that unlocks one will never unlock any other in the set. But, if carefully conceived, there is often one separate *special* key that can open them all.

At the top of the deceptively simple drawing are the words— SKELETON KEY.

Jack trains her eyes on the paper, her brow furrowed in concentration, and again I see her lips move as she sounds out every letter. She gasps when she understands.

I put my finger to my lips again, fold up the design, and

put it firmly in her palm. Then I take the spare bit of paper and charcoal again and write— *you make it alone.*

Jack reads my words slowly and then looks at her sleeping father. I touch her arm and shake my head. Then I point at her and mouth the word— *you*.

Her big eyes swim with fear. I meet her gaze with trust. It could go either way, really. She could buckle under the pressure. I might be asking too much, but I don't think I am. And I'm right.

Jack doesn't rush in. She doesn't immediately agree. She thinks about it. She thinks about how she would do it behind everyone's backs. And when she's figured out how—like I knew she would—she nods once, and the designs disappear somewhere under the layers of clothes she wears to bind and cover the curves and dips that are starting to form on her.

I smile at her, relieved. Then I write— *memorize the design, then burn it.*

She half nods, half shrugs like she already knew that.

I write— *you are my secret apprentice now.*

She looks at me, torn between fear and excitement. She shakes her head and writes back— *I cant*, in shaky letters.

Why? Because you don't want me to find out that you're a girl? I write.

I wait for her to read it. When I see her tumultuous expression, I get up, crossing to the fires of the forge to burn the spare bit of paper we used to write our conversation. I hold it over the flame, waiting for her agreement, but also showing that she and I both have secrets that could be used against us. Unless I burn them. It's up to her, really.

She gives me a wry smile. After deliberating carefully, she nods in agreement.

I throw the paper into the fire and let it burn, keeping my end of the bargain.

With that settled, I go back outside to look for Dragon. I was expecting him to come in as a man at some point during that exchange with Jack, but he didn't. I go out back to see him still in his draconian form, stubbornly atop what's left of his hoard.

"It's not going anywhere, Dragon," I say, sighing. "No one knows it's here. No one's going to steal what they don't know about."

Dragon huffs smoke out his nose and curls tighter around his hoard.

"Intolerable beast." I yawn and stretch. "Well, I must sleep," I say, turning. "Good night, Dragon."

I hear his wing unfurl, and it appears in front of me like a net and catches me. I turn back to him. His emerald eyes are two glowing slits in the dark.

"I don't want to mislead you. Again," I say, thinking of earlier in his cave.

He blows a gust of hot air at me, sending my hair and my skirts flying in a way that can only be comical, and I can't help but laugh.

"You're going to make me sleep outside, aren't you?" I ask, grinning at him. His eyes slide closed until they are lambent slits. "Well, open your claw so I may get in." I nudge one of his enormous talons with my hip as he refolds his wing.

Dragon opens his claw and lets me climb into his grasp. I

yawn hugely, I'm so tired. "This is unnecessary, you know," I say.

He grouses as if to say *my gold.* Or, *my bed.* I can't tell the difference, really. It might just be that dragons prefer sleeping on gold to anything else. Whatever it is, he's decided it's his and he won't move his silly head off it for the world.

"You can always make more," I remind him.

Sparks come out of Dragon's nose, making me laugh.

I'm too sleepy to argue with Draconian Dragon. That usually involves me getting snatched up and flown to some gorgeous yet strange location, and I need actual rest. I unlace my kirtle and stow Dragonbarb in my garter. I take off my boots, unbraid my hair, and slip down further into the hollow of Dragon's claw. He watches me with his glowing emerald eyes.

"Good night, Dragon," I murmur, snuggling against his warm scales. He cages me safely in the palm of his hand, and I sleep.

But only for an hour or so. Morning arrives much too soon, and with it comes Mistress Waverly. I hear her voice waking everyone inside the forge. I sit up inside Dragon's opening claw as she joins us outside with a basket held in the crook of her arm.

"Oh my," she gasps. She stares at Dragon unabashedly for just a moment, but quickly remembers her manners and gives him a respectful curtsy and a bright smile. "My lord." She turns to me. "You slept well, I hope, milady."

She holds out a hand to help steady me as I climb out of Dragon's claw.

"The only thing my sleep lacked was duration," I assure

her. I respect her for her tact. Though I'm sure she's helped ladies arise from strange beds before, I'll wager never one quite like this.

She helps me into my kirtle without waiting for me to ask, and she even braids my hair with sure hands while I lace on my boots and tighten my garter around Dragonbarb.

"I've brought breakfast for everyone," Mistress Waverly says, but then she frowns suddenly, appraising Dragon's enormousness. "Although I don't think it will be enough for you as you are, milord. I could procure you either several young goats or one old steer. Or all of them, if you please."

Dragon grumble-laughs and stands to stretch. As he does so, gold spills out from between his scales.

"Careful there." I take Mistress Waverly by the shoulder and steer her away, lest she be injured by falling coin. "Lord Dragon will be a man in a moment and join us for a regular breakfast," I tell her.

Dragon unfurls his wings and lets his long tongue spill out between his arsenal of teeth in a yawn. "Such a showman, isn't he, Mistress?" I say teasingly, though the look on her face is one of pure awe. "Come on, we'd best get inside and let him change."

She glances over her shoulder once as we cross the courtyard. From the way she startles and spins around to face the front, I'm certain Dragon has shifted into his human form. Mistress Waverly looks at me, eyes wide.

"Oh my," she murmurs.

"Yes, I know," I agree sadly.

She looks at me, confused. "But he is your intended, is he not?"

"No." I shake my head. "I was given to him, but that was more of a culinary arrangement, rather than a *marital* one."

Her lips are pursed, and her eyes are narrowed in disbelief.

"It's true," I own. "I'm helping him recover his name, and then we go our separate ways."

She makes a *harrumphing* sound. "As you say, milady," she replies and leaves it at that.

The rest of our party is rising slowly and shuffling to the main drafting table. Jack clears off all the drawings and stacks them neatly on the shelves while Mistress Waverly and Limond lay out the food and bring around extra chairs.

Dragon comes in through the back door. He's carrying two sacks of gold in each hand. Putter and Lakonius hurry to help him.

"Here, allow me, Lord Dragon," Putter says, trying to take a sack out of Dragon's hand.

Dragon gives him a funny look, and then when he finally relents and lets Putter have the sack, Putter can't so much as slow its descent to the floor.

Putter bends over and tries to lift the sack. But for all his heaving he can't do more than make the gold inside jingle.

"I'll carry," Dragon says softly. He lifts the sack easily, brings it and the other three bags across the room, and sets all of them down near the finished lockboxes.

Everyone is staring at him, of course, marveling at his strength. He shifts from foot to foot, and his eyes find mine anxiously. He loathes being the center of attention, I've noticed.

"It appears one needs the strength of a Dragon Lord to

carry a dragon's hoard. Probably why I've been destitute my whole life," I say broadly. That gets a laugh and draws eyes away from Dragon. "Come, everyone, sit and eat. Though, Jack? I want you to go out and help Lord Dragon by scouring the courtyard for any loose coins."

Jack scurries after Dragon with bright eyes. They've not even gotten to the door before Jack starts haranguing him with questions.

"Do you need to eat coal to breathe fire?" she asks.

Dragon's deep laugh rumbles in the air and in the floor beneath. He rubs Jack's short, spiky hair fondly and replies quietly, "Must you swallow m-music to sing?"

They move out of earshot before I can hear any more, though I wish I could ask all the questions Jack is asking as unabashedly as she does. As everyone else sits down to eat, a young boy comes running into the forge.

"There's a lord waiting for Lady Jonara at the Inn!" the boy puffs breathlessly.

"Glomsby?" I ask though I know it shouldn't be him. It's too early for his return unless there was some mishap.

The boy shrugs emphatically. "I dunno. He paid me a copper and told me he needs to speak to you alone."

I excuse myself and hasten back to the inn. There is no one in the tavern waiting for me, or indeed anyone downstairs at all. I figure there must have been a mistake.

"Hello?" I call out, and I think I hear someone replying from upstairs, but the voice is both agitated and muffled. I mount the stairs. As I am walking down the hallway toward the sound, I hear someone behind me.

"*Lady* Jonara," says the voice in scoffing tones.

I turn, suddenly aware of how quiet it is at the inn today. I see a familiar, but not a friendly, face.

"Barth?" I ask. "What are you—"

I don't get a chance to finish. Two men appear out of the room next to me. They grab each of my arms. Before I can scream, Barth puts a black bag over my head.

16

Of course, I struggle. I shout, though my voice is muffled by the bag. I buck and twist, planting my feet and using my strong legs. I throw at least two of my assailants to the ground, but I am seized again and lifted off my feet before I manage to get away.

Despite my crazed efforts, they carry me down what I assume are the back stairs, through what smells like the kitchen, and into a waiting carriage behind the inn. I am shoved down onto the floor of the carriage and covered by a blanket. The horses are kept to a sedate pace for a few moments, probably to avoid drawing too much attention while we are in the town center, but it doesn't take long before they are whipped into a run.

The whole incident couldn't have taken them more than a few minutes, and I am well and truly abducted.

"Where are you taking me?" I ask when my voice is steady enough to speak.

"How do you know we're taking you anywhere?" Barth replies, sniggering. "What if we're just planning to have our way with you?"

"Are you really that thick?" I snap. Can't help it. He's an idiot. "If you were going to do that you'd have done it at the inn. Push me into my room. Lock the door. You know."

"How do you know we're not just going to kill you?" asks one of the other ruffians.

I sigh. "Again, you would have done it straight away. A quick rape or murder, and you could split up and take your chances. With multiple trails to follow you might be the one that gets away. But abducting me and staying in a group is risky. Lord Dragon will come looking for me." I pause and let that sink in for a moment. "And when he finds me, he'll kill you all."

"Maybe we should rethink this," a second ruffian mumbles. He sounds older than Barth or the first ruffian.

"Yeah, you said the Dragon Lord wouldn't care!" a third squeaks. He sounds much younger than all of them.

"She's lying. Why would a Dragon Lord waste his time looking for a tinker's daughter?" Barth says, tittering nervously.

"Because I belong to him. I was given to him as a sacrifice," I reply. "He took me and put me on top of his hoard. Haven't you ever heard what a dragon does to men who steal from his hoard?"

"Shut it!" Barth barks, kicking me for good measure.

"Here now. You never said anything about her belonging to him!" the first ruffian shouts. This one chafes under

Barth's leadership. Maybe he believes he should have been put in charge.

"We should give her back," the third ruffian says—the young one. He's a bit jumpy. "Just let her out with the bag on her head. She hasn't seen most of us."

"It's too late for that," Barth says, snapping under the pressure.

"You know what a dragon can do?" asks the young one in a shrill voice.

"You know what Asphodel will do if we let her go!?" Barth yells back. That silences them.

"Ohh," I say, drawing out the word. "You're taking me to Asphodel."

Barth kicks me again. "I told you to shut it!" he snarls. He's irate now, more with his own mistakes than with me, I'd wager, but I'm handy and utterly kickable given my current condition.

"You don't have to be so rough with her," the older ruffian protests. He's soft-hearted. Probably has a daughter my age.

"Didn't Asphodel say she was not to be harmed?" the first ruffian asks tauntingly. He's challenging Barth's leadership. All of them are, but him the most. If I could but speak to him without Barth present, I might be able to stick a knife of mutiny into the crack between them and twist it.

A knife. Dragonbarb! I've grown so accustomed to the feel of it in my garter that I'd almost forgotten it was there. But there are four of them in here with me, and at least one more driving the carriage. That's too many. I need to wait for a better opportunity. I need to *make* a better opportunity.

We rattle along for a while. I can smell pine sap and loam. They are taking me into the wildwood.

"There's another option," I say.

"I told you—" Barth begins, but number one stops him.

"Let her talk."

"You can turn this carriage around and go back to Lord Dragon," I say. "He can protect you from Asphodel—and he's rich. He's sure to reward you in gold, or even pay you a handsome wage, should you join him."

"Why would he let us join him? Why would he do anything other than kill us?" the first ruffian asks.

"Lord Dragon punishes the wrongs done against him, but you haven't done anything wrong yet. I'm all in one piece, and ready to forgive and forget if it benefits my Lord Dragon for me to do so," I say. "You've proved you are men of action, and therefore useful. And you may very well have information about Asphodel that Lord Dragon needs."

There is silence. They are considering my offer.

I am suddenly thrown across the floor of the carriage as the horses are brought to an abrupt halt. The ruffians curse and brace themselves, and at least one of them falls on top of me. Clearly, they were not expecting this to stop any more than I was.

Stunned and tumbled witless, we hear the driver jump down and come around to the door of the carriage.

"What the bloody hell is wrong with you!?" Barth shouts at him.

"You have failed me," the driver says in a silky voice. "You will feel pain now."

Barth starts shrieking at the top of his lungs. The sound is high, shrill, and intolerable. I can't imagine what kind of torment he is suffering if even the sound is so unbearable. When I don't think I can take it a second longer, he throws himself from the carriage and runs away.

"Let's see what's under the blanket," says the silky voice. I feel the fresh air hit my flushed skin as the blanket is pulled away. "Sit up and remove the hood," the voice orders.

I do as the voice says and must blink my eyes at the light. At first, I see a plain-looking man crouched over me, but as I regard him, his face changes utterly. It is no trick of the light or a distortion created by my sun-startled eyes. This is magic.

He becomes the second most beautiful man I have ever seen, but no man could be more different from Dragon than this. Fair skin and black hair hover over me like a face chipped from the moon and framed in midnight. His hazel eyes slide closed as he takes a deep breath, smelling me. Trapped under a blanket, the spicy, smoky smell of Dragon must have grown quite powerful.

"You are obviously very special to him," the man says. His voice practically purrs. He looks down at my bare arms and my eyes follow his, seeing what he sees. Dusted with gold, my skin glistens like a pile of coin. "He's perfumed and gilded you like a queen, and with good cause. In just a few minutes of talking you nearly turned these men against me. How did you manage that?"

Though Barth's screams still reverberate in the woods around us, I swallow and slow my sprinting fear. I narrow my eyes at him.

"You embedded yourself with them in disguise, I assume to watch their every move, and you wonder how *I* turned them?" I ask, carefully treading the thin line between honesty and insolence.

He breathes out a surprised laugh. "I suppose distrust is repaid in kind." He turns suddenly and yells over his shoulder. "Oh, do shut up, Barth! You sound like a squealing pig." The sounds of agony cease. Asphodel turns back to me. "I can't abide feckless men. You can't even torture them without it being torturous for all." He looks over his shoulder again. "Well? Get in here."

Asphodel backs out of the carriage with balance and ease —never taking his eyes off me—as Barth shrinks past his master to climb inside. Pale, shaking, and sweating, Barth presses himself into the farthest corner away from Asphodel. He clearly wishes he could run away, and yet his body is doing something other than he wants.

I look around at the rest of the ruffians and see that they are unnaturally still. They look as if they'd been trapped in amber. They are all straining in their muscles to move, but unable to do so. I know most magic is illusion and completely in the mind, but the mind rules the body, and right now it does not seem as if any of the men in this carriage are in control of their own faculties.

"Please, my lady," Asphodel says, gesturing to the seats.

I get off the floor and slide onto one of the seats, pausing every now and again to make sure that I am in charge of my movement, and not the puppet of a sorcerer.

"I suggest you hold on to something tightly, my lady, for

I believe a dragon will soon be following us," Asphodel says, and then he closes the carriage door.

We ride at a full gallop, all of us thrown hither and thither about the inside of the coach, for about half of an hour more. Asphodel pulls the horses to an abrupt halt alongside another coach and driver. He vaults from the top of one carriage to the other. Hanging over the side so that he never sets a foot to the ground, he opens the doors.

"Jump," he tells the ruffians, and one by one they jump from one coach to the other until I am left alone.

"Get under the blanket, my lady, and remove your dress," he tells me.

"I will do no such thing," I reply coldly.

Holding a parcel, he vaults from the top of the other carriage onto mine, and then swings himself in through the open door, as lithe as an acrobat. He stands over me, and I push myself away, but I keep my chin up defiantly.

"No one will watch you, my lady. I will make certain of it. But I do need you to leave that dragon-scented dress in this carriage." His eyes narrow and one side of his expressive mouth curves up in a taunting smile. "You may either remove the dress yourself or I will rip it off you."

Asphodel looms over me for a moment. We glare at each other. And then he pointedly turns his back to me.

I'm not an idiot. I realize that in a battle of wills against Asphodel, this is the best deal I'm going to get. Besides, if he does as he threatened and tears my clothes off, he'll find Dragonbarb. I hastily start unlacing my kirtle, but I keep my garters and Dragonbarb well under the blanket as I disrobe.

When I've got my dress off, Asphodel reaches his arm back without turning around and passes me the parcel.

"Put this on," he says.

I unfurl a length of wine-red velvet to discover that it is a lovely gown. Quite possibly the nicest I've ever seen in my life, and far better than anything I'd ever hoped to wear.

"Hurry. And try not to get too much dragon scent on it," Asphodel says impatiently.

"It's not like I can help it," I snap, muffled under the luxurious fabric. I try to lace myself up hastily, but it ties at the back, rather than the front like my kirtle. I get as far as I can on my own, but this gown simply wasn't made for the class of people who dress themselves.

"I don't know why you thought this was the proper dress to bring, but it's a two-person job. You'll have to help me, or I'll be indecent," I tell Asphodel.

"Right. I'm turning around," he announces, which is astonishingly respectful. And a far cry from ripping my clothes off me.

A ruffian, I can handle. A gentleman, I can handle. A man who is both and neither is unsettling. I clasp the bodice to me, so it doesn't fall when I stand, and swing my waist-long hair around and over my shoulder as I give him my back. His fingers are cool against the bare skin at the bottom of my spine as he gathers the laces and starts to thread them through.

"You're painted with gold," he grumbles. "I should soak you in a tub and strain your bath water. It'd pay my army for a month."

"Yes, by all means. Let's stop here and I'll take a lengthy

bath, waiting for my Lord Dragon to come and heat the water for me." I guffaw. "After he chars the meat off your bones."

I can sense Asphodel smiling behind me. I don't know how I can feel a smile I can't see, but I can feel his. Maybe it's because he's a sorcerer.

"There's even gold behind your *ears*," Asphodel mutters disbelievingly. He pulls the laces tight. "Can't quite work out how you managed that."

"I don't know what you're insinuating," I say defensively. "But if you must know, Dragon gets itchy. As his sacrifice, it's my duty and privilege to scratch him."

"And do you scratch him with your ears?"

It's his tone that makes me laugh, as much as what he says. I feel Asphodel's breath of answering laughter against the back of my neck, and it's not unpleasant. Which is disconcerting. He quickly ties off the top of my corset and steps back. When I turn around, I can't meet his gaze.

"We tarry too long," he says. He can't meet my gaze, either, I realize. "Do you need my assistance or are you able to jump across?" he asks quietly. This has suddenly become terribly uncomfortable for us both.

"I can manage," I say, holding up my skirts, and I leap across the gap to the other carriage.

Asphodel vaults from the doorway of the old carriage, briefly grabs onto the top of the doorway of the new carriage, and then swings himself up onto the roof in a series of motions I cannot describe as anything but elegant.

As Asphodel slides across the roof of the new carriage, the driver quits his seat and jumps across. The driver takes the old carriage and my heavily perfumed dress back the way we came. Asphodel takes us on a perpendicular route to the one that we had been following.

Any scent trail that Dragon might be following to find me is now either hopelessly muddled or completely lost.

17

I do not try to plead with the ruffians crammed into the back of the carriage with me. They seem stiff, as if their bodies and minds still do not belong to them. Yet, even if they could move of their own volition, I hold out no hope of convincing them to help me escape—not since witnessing what happened to Barth.

After what I believe to be another two hours of pushing the horses to their limit, we leave the forest and enter a clearing along the bank of a river. We pass through wooden spikes sticking out of the ground, demarcating a fortified encampment.

Inside the hastily laid defenses, there are about twenty tents each of them large enough to bunk ten men at least. Dotted between the tents are raised platforms, upon which six or seven men scan the skies.

Asphodel pulls the horses up and jumps down from the driver's seat with the same acrobatic grace he exhibited on the roofs of the carriages. A knight wearing chainmail under a cloak approaches Asphodel and stands sharply at attention. On the shoulder of his cloak is a hydra crest.

"I bought some time with her dress. That may throw him off the trail." Asphodel bites his lower lip in thought and looks at me through the carriage window. "But he'll come," he says. "Please escort Lady Jonara to my tent. And put those men in the stocks."

"Yes, Lord Asphodel," the knight replies, waving four more soldiers forward to assist him.

As Asphodel walks out of sight, Barth and the rest of the ruffians seem to be released from whatever paralytic hold Asphodel had over them. They startle and gain possession of their own limbs, just as the soldiers take hold of them and drag them from the carriage, kicking and screaming. The knight remains with me and waits for the commotion to die down before he addresses me.

"If you would be so kind as to quit the carriage, milady," the knight says. His tone is solicitous, yet his hand is on the pommel of his broadsword.

"Sir--?" I inquire politely as I lay my hand on the mail of his proffered arm.

"Sir Lakely," he replies.

"You know your name," I say. I step down.

"Yes, milady," Sir Lakely says. "A war cannot be fought by witless men. I know of what I speak. I used to serve our departed king and he left this land in shambles."

We walk alongside each other, looking for all the world like we are amiable companions. "For some reason, I'd thought, or maybe just hoped, that anyone who followed

Asphodel did so because they had been ensorcelled in some way."

Sir Lakely lets out a surprised laugh. "You are forthcoming with your opinions. I respect that, but you do this land a discredit if you discount Lord Asphodel."

I turn to Sir Lakely, my expression openly astonished. "Please, do tell, after seeing that he has robbed town after town of their minds and souls, how *else* I should count Lord Asphodel?"

"He is the most brilliant leader I've ever known," Sir Lakely replies without hesitation. "He is organized, focused, talented, and decisive. All of these traits would make him a great king, and this land *needs* a king, milady. Every town he comes to, he asks that they swear loyalty to him and declare him king before he invades. Those who resist are punished, of course. But that is the way of war."

We stop. We have come to an unremarkable, if only slightly larger tent than the others, that I'm assuming is Asphodel's. I meet Sir Lakely's eyes.

"You are right on many counts, good Sir Knight. Lord Asphodel has all of the traits that would mark him as a great king, and our land desperately needs one," I say, releasing Lakely's forearm. "But after seeing for myself what Asphodel has done, I could never call him my king."

Sir Lakely nods. "You are too young to have ever seen the face of war, but I have seen it, and so I must ask you. Is taking a name worse than taking a life? A name can be restored, but a life cannot. As far as conquerors go, Lord Asphodel is far kinder than the ones I've known."

I smile at him, for I see now that he is an honest man who is trying to do the right thing.

"And I would agree with you, Sir Lakely," I reply. "If—and only if—Asphodel intended to restore the names he's taken. If not, he's not only killed all those people but he's done it slowly and without honor."

Sir Lakely bows to me, but he is frowning as he thinks over my words. "Milady," he says, giving me leave.

"Good Sir Knight," I reply, curtsying. I enter Asphodel's quarters, leaving Sir Lakely to turn over his troubled thoughts alone.

Asphodel's tent is a basic arrangement with no extra frills. There's a cot for a bed, a simple basin, and a pitcher for a bath. There's also a spare outfit consisting of a doublet and breeches held up by some unseen rack. The one luxury it seems Asphodel has afforded himself is the extensive desk and the mounds of parchment scattered around it. It looks as if Asphodel had been pulling the leaves out of a folio, desperately searching for something.

My gait stiffens as I near the desk and the shapes on the pieces of parchment become clear to me. The drawings are all designs for warded locks.

I bend over the drawings, recognizing them. One is from Master Yokum the Elder. I studied his designs at length when I was learning how to build warded locks. The other two are designs of mine from not that long ago. I stare at them in disbelief. Not only was I unaware that these drawings still existed, but that Asphodel was studying them seems unreal.

Something moves in the corner where there were only clothes a moment ago. I jump back from Asphodel's desk.

The doublet and breeches are walking toward me, but there is no rack inside them. There is no man inside of them either, though the clothes are moving as if a body inhabits them. My breath catches and flutters hysterically in my chest.

When I can finally breathe again, I scream and run for the door. I careen headlong into Asphodel's arms as he enters.

"Run!" I yell into his face.

Asphodel draws his sword as he puts me behind him, inspecting his quarters. I grab onto his tunic and feel his muscles bunch as he drops into a fighting crouch.

"What has frightened you so?" he asks after a moment.

"Ghost!" I hiss, pointing around his shoulder at the apparition.

He deflates suddenly, and tries to turn and face me, though I still cling to his shirt. "My lady, that is no ghost. That's my manservant. You have nothing to fear." He sheathes his sword.

"Any moment now it will attack and suck out our insides through our noses," I whisper, staring at it.

"He will do no such—" Asphodel begins. His expression changes suddenly. He's trying not to laugh as he asks, "Why through our *noses*?"

"My father said that's how ghosts do it!" I reply.

"Well, he's not a ghost." Asphodel sighs and turns to the haunted clothing. "Leave us. You're upsetting Lady Jonara."

The doublet bows and exits the tent.

I give it a wide berth, just in case. Then I realize I'm biting something I shouldn't be biting. I unclasp my hands and release the mouthful of Asphodel's linen shirt I had been masticating. I step back. Asphodel is regarding me strangely.

"What?" I finally say when the silence has dragged on for too long.

He shakes his head, looking bemused. "You consort with dragons, fight your kidnappers like a demon, face a sorcerer with defiance, but a pair of breeches, a doublet, and a cravat scares you?"

"I don't like ghosts," I say primly as I smooth my skirts. "My father told me a ghost story when I was small. It gave me nightmares for weeks."

"It's a good thing ghosts aren't real, then," he replies, smiling at me with narrowed eyes.

"That's what my father said, but he usually has the wrong end of the stick about things." I look away, aware that I'm nattering on. I keep nattering, though, because I'm nervous. "He even thinks fairies are real." My gaze drifts over to his desk. Asphodel marks my change in attention and his demeanor hardens.

"My manservant told me you were looking through my papers," he says crisply as he goes behind his desk.

"It spoke to you?"

"Only I can see or hear him." He gestures to the seat across his desk. "Please. Do sit."

I take the folding chair across from him, but my thoughts are still on the apparition.

"This design of yours is of interest to me. I haven't been able to engineer a skeleton key out of it."

I glance briefly at the design and give him a curt smile. "Nor will you," I say, and then get back to the apparition.

"So, there is a living man inside the clothes, yet no one but you can see or hear him? How awful for him. How long has he served you?"

Asphodel sighs and leans back in his chair. He throws my design onto his desk and regards me in a measuring way for a few moments.

"I stopped counting the lifetimes," he finally replies.

"Lifetimes?" I breathe, wondering how old Asphodel must be. "And how long will he be enslaved?"

I see a muscle in his jaw jump as he clenches his teeth. "As long as I am."

I tilt toward him across the desk. "How are *you* enslaved?" I ask.

He has no reason to answer me, and I am a little surprised when he does.

"I can't die, to some extent," he says softly. "My body stops working, everything goes dark, and I go away for a while... but I always come back. When I do, it's like I'm starting in the middle of... something. Never at the beginning, which I can't remember." A desperate look steals across his face, and I feel pain for him, yet when Asphodel looks up at me again his eyes are cold. "All I know is that my manservant is to blame, so that is his punishment." He picks up my drawing and puts it in my hand. "Now. Why can't I devise a skeleton key for this? Everything mechanical has a solution, except your locks."

"You'll be able to devise a key for each individual lock by studying each design, but in order to make the skeleton key, you'd need all of the designs. But I always omit one lock in a series. I simply don't make it, but the step is still there in the subsequent locks. Which means one step will always be missing. That's why you'll never figure it out."

"Brilliant," he whispers.

I shake my head, holding the design limply in my hand. I can't seem to let go of this manservant business.

"Back to my questions though," I say, smiling because I know I'm pushing my luck. "What did your manservant do to you?"

"I can't remember," he answers curtly. "This new series of lockboxes you've conceived for your Dragon Lord— have you designed the skeleton key yet?"

"Yes," I reply. "How do you know your manservant deserves this punishment if you can't remember what he did?"

"How do you know you're in love with your Dragon Lord?" he snaps. "Do you remember exactly what he did that earned your love?"

"No," I reply quietly. And there it is. I love Dragon, though I don't think I knew it until I heard Asphodel say it. "But I love him all the same."

"Hate is remarkably similar to love. It binds you to another."

I laugh. "I don't think you've ever been in love, then."

"Why is that?"

"Love doesn't bind you," I reply, thinking of all the things I've done and felt since I first laid eyes on Dragon's big golden head.

"No?" Asphodel challenges.

"No." Whenever I think of Dragon, I think of shackles falling away. "It sets you free," I say, shrugging.

"Does it?" Asphodel narrows his eyes at me. "I'm going to be frank with you. My bid for the crown urgently requires funds, and my coffers are dangerously low. You've lined your lockboxes with dragon scales. Did you know that dragon scales are impervious to spells?"

I nod my head and swallow to speak. "They aren't impervious, though."

"Nothing is," he agrees. "But it would take me weeks to get inside them. Weeks I don't have before my army deserts." He pauses for effect. "I need the skeleton key and I need it now."

"I don't have it," I reply honestly.

"Where is it?" The smile he gives me is brittle, and I remember Barth's shrieks.

Suddenly, a very different Asphodel is sitting before me. This is not the same man who laced my dress, or who rushed into the tent in my defense when he heard me scream. It's as if another man has been painted on top of him, and this Asphodel is terrifying.

I shake my head, though I know what it might mean for me. "I won't tell you."

"And why not? For love?"

I smile wryly. Again, Asphodel has revealed my own feelings to me, yet in this instance, he is mistaken about who those feelings are for. Jack is the one with the skeleton key, and I would never betray her.

"Yes," I reply.

Asphodel's face darkens, and he stands from his chair. He takes my arm and hauls me up, pulling me out of his tent. "I'm going to show you where love leads you, and you tell me whether or not it *sets you free*," he repeats, mocking me.

Asphodel marches me past the raised platforms, but they look different from when we first rode into the encampment. Now they are topped with dragon bows. I count fifteen raised platforms, each one armed and manned by a team of ten men. All of the dragon bows are angled upward.

This is not an encampment. It's a trap, and I'm the bait.

I don't try to fight or run away. Even if I were to run, Dragon would still come here to follow my scent. I don't resist, yet Asphodel still holds my arm tight enough to leave bruises as he drags me past the dragon bows and toward an enormous willow tree by the side of the rushing river.

"Very shortly, your Dragon Lord will come flying here looking for you, and when he does, I'm going to shoot him in the heart."

He pulls me closer to him for one moment, his anger ebbing and his eyes echoing my sadness. It's almost as if he's remembered feeling the same pain I'm feeling now, and again I get a glimpse of the real man beneath the evil paint. But then the tide of rage rushes back in on him as if it comes not from him, but from an outside source. He roughly pushes me toward the willow tree.

"That's what love gets you," he says bitterly.

I stumble and fall at the base of the tree, only to see that something is chained to the other side of the trunk. I realize it's a man, pressed tight to the bark. The chains seem to burn his skin, and the bark is tearing holes in his thin, iridescent wings.

He's got iridescent wings.

"Tie her up with him!" Asphodel yells at the nearest man-at-arms. The soldier scurries forward and pins me to the tree.

Asphodel pushes his beautiful face close to mine. "You are an exceptionally clever woman, Lady Jonara, but you are wrong on two counts. Love is but a trap. And fairies are in fact, real."

He turns and leaves me to be tied to the willow tree with a real fairy.

18

The fairy waits until the men-at-arms move off enough that they are out of earshot.

"I've never seen Asphodel that angry," he says. "What did you do to get such a rise out of him?"

We sit back-to-back with the tree trunk between us. The fairy is facing the river, while I face the camp and the guards. I tip my head to the side to answer him.

"I said no," I reply in a listless voice.

"Oh, darling, why? He's gorgeous," the fairy replies effervescently. "Sure, he's evil and all that. He's chained me in *iron* to a *willow* tree— can't tell you how uncomfortable both of those things are for a fairy— but I'd probably still give him a tumble if he asked."

Though I'm downtrodden in every sense of the word, I can't help but laugh in surprise. "He didn't proposition me in *that* way," I reply, scandalized.

"He never does, I've noticed. Always sleeps alone, that

one. Very sad," the fairy says, tisking. "Evil and sad. What a depressing combination. Such a luscious waste." Again, I laugh at the fairy's audacity, though I have no idea how he can be so jovial whilst his skin is smoking. "So how did you get him that angry? It's not like him to become emotional."

There's no reason not to tell him. It's not a secret. "He demanded I give him the skeleton key to the lockboxes I designed for the Dragon Lord."

I hear the fairy's sharp intake of breath. "Oh. That's you then?" he asks, his tone turning serious.

"I'm Jonara. Everyone's calling me Lady Jonara, but I'm not a lady," I admit. "I'm a tinker's daughter. I'm quite handy at fixing things and building small mechanisms. And I'm especially good at designing locks."

"First of all, every woman is a lady if she acts like one," he says emphatically. "Come to think of it, every man is too. Second, you are not a tinker's daughter if you do the tinkering. You are a tinker. Lastly... I forgot what my last point was going to be."

"What's your name?" I prompt.

"I am Bixel."

"I didn't think fairies were real," I say.

"Darling, I never believed in myself either, and then when I was about a hundred and fifty, I realized that I was wasting my time decorating the fairy court with my astonishing good looks, if I may be so bold. That was right around the time Asphodel started abducting fairies and stealing their magic— insufferable sorcerer. So, I decided to get off my impeccable derriere and use my extraordinary talents. And now I'm finally living up to my full potential!"

"Yes, I've noticed. You're of so much use tied to this tree," I tease, enjoying his lighthearted banter, though it has drawn the attention of the guards and they are starting to move closer to us.

"Ironically, yes, and to *you*, in fact." His voice drops. "I know your Dragon Lord's name."

The men-at-arms come and loom over us for a few moments and we are forced to halt our conversation momentarily.

"How?" I whisper as soon as the guards have moved away again. "How do you remember it if it hasn't been given back to him yet? Do you have it written down?"

"I'm a *fairy*, dear," he replies like it's obvious. "Unlike human sorcerers who can only do real magic by half killing themselves, real magic is mine to wield. In fact, Asphodel has been using my magic to cast his name-stealing spell on entire towns and stay vital. Hence, my current state as an abject prisoner with no strength to fight the sapping of an ever-thirsty willow."

"Tell me his name," I beg.

"Won't do you any good. I could say it a thousand times but it wouldn't stick in your head until someone gives his name back to him."

"Write it down. I can read."

"Yes, a bit hard to do at the present moment."

I lean my head back against the tree trunk. My gaze floats up to the sky. Please, Dragon. Don't come. Don't save me.

"You must escape for two reasons," I whisper. "First, you must deprive Asphodel of his power to cast his name-stealing spell on anyone else. Second, you must get to Dragon and give him back his name, so he can face Asphodel and defeat him."

Bixel makes a wise sound. "Yes, I must. But unfortunately, I'm drained of magic at the moment and chained to a tree. Also, a bit peckish, to be honest."

I thunk the back of my head against the tree trunk. The action, though painful, dislodges an idea. "Can you reach back around the trunk and get under my skirts?" I ask.

"Definitely. But— please don't take offense, as I find your company delightful— but what's under your skirts isn't in my area of *interest*."

"Not even if it's a dragon blade that can cut through iron?"

There's a slight pause. "That does change things a bit."

I hear him grunt and shuffle as he tries to scoot around the base of the tree and get closer to me. I try to scoot closer to him as well. I swing my leg to the side as far as it will go.

"Flexible, aren't you? I can see why *merfme* is taken with you," Bixel says as his hand travels up and down my thigh.

"Lower," I direct. "Wait. Did you just say Dragon's name?"

"Yes. But it probably sounded like gibberish to you. That must be difficult when you care about someone," Bixel says, sadly.

"Is he... you know... married?" I ask hesitantly. I don't know if I want to know. "Does he have children?"

"Of course not. He's barely five and twenty." I feel him latch onto my garter. "Got it!"

He starts to pull out Dragonbarb. "No, you'll have to take the sheath, too," I tell him. "You'll cut yourself to ribbons without it." Bixel curses and fumbles with my garter. "Everyone in my last village was married by sixteen," I continue. "Except me, of course."

"I assure you, where *merfme* is from, they don't tend to marry whilst still teenagers." I feel the garter loosen.

"So, he's unmarried," I say, but the thought brings regret, not happiness. I feel my garter come off, but unfortunately, it's gone to the wrong man.

"Never taken a garter off before and I'll never do it again. That was horrid." Bixel says, groaning with relief.

"The sun is setting," I say. "In about half an hour, it will be dark enough for you to cut yourself free and run for it. Get to Bolloxville and give Dragon back his name."

"I notice you said *you* and not *we*. You're coming with me," Bixel says sternly.

"With both of us gone, Asphodel is sure to notice immediately. But if I stay, you have a chance to get away."

Bixel makes a frustrated sound. "My dear, you are far too valiant for your own good."

"It's not valiant to understand that if we both go, we both get caught," I reply. "I'm facing the camp while you're partially hidden by the tree. And I'm in a red dress. I won't get ten paces before they notice."

"True," Bixel says musingly. "Though you do look ravishing in red." He becomes serious again. "You've saved my life, milady, and that puts me in your debt. I shall serve you until that debt is paid. I'll come back for you," he promises. "Please remember that, in case Asphodel..."

"Yes," I say hastily before my courage fails. I try not to recall Barth's screams, but they are fresh in my mind.

We sit in silence as the sun sets and shadows descend around us in foggy fingers. As the last bit of light leaves the sky, Asphodel comes to our tree. He paces in front of me for a few moments, hands on his hips as if I had promised him something that didn't happen. I smile when I realize that sunset means Asphodel may have missed his chance. They can't shoot Dragon from the sky if they can't see him.

"Where is your Lord Dragon?" Asphodel says in a loud and challenging voice. "Where is your love?"

"Don't engage him," Bixel whispers to me in warning.

Asphodel paces in front of me, every pass building his intensity. "Does it hurt, to realize that he didn't care enough to come to your rescue?" he asks.

I shake my head. "I don't want to be saved," I say.

Asphodel comes nearer, his face softening, but I can't figure out his expression. It's almost as if he both loves me and hates me.

"I'd come for you, even if it meant my death," he says, his eyes scanning over my face rather than looking into mine. "He thinks he's smart. He's learned that he can't fly during the day. But what he doesn't realize, is that I've learned to see in the dark." Asphodel turns and stalks off, yelling, "Light the torches!"

Bixel waits until the men-at-arms move away from us to light the torches. "He's positively *vexed*. What did you do to him?" he asks.

"Nothing!" I insist. I'm puzzled myself. "You'd better go while the guards are busy with the torches." My suggestion is met with silence.

"Bixel?" I turn to the side and feel the chains slacken.

He's already cut himself free and run for it with Dragonbarb. Or flown for it. Not sure how fairies flee, actually. It seems as if he went across the river which is too rapid to wade across. I'm glad his wings are well enough to fly.

I deflate, feeling smaller now that I'm alone and deprived of Bixel's irreverent humor, but I take heart in the knowledge that he can help Dragon, even if I can't.

Many torches are lit, and there is a bright glow about the camp, but the sky is still dark. I hear chanting. The torches begin to go out one by one and a sphere of light starts to shine around Asphodel. I can see him standing in the middle of the camp as if he were standing under a dome of daylight. The dome begins to grow out and up until the whole camp and the sky above it looks as if it were the middle of the afternoon. The dome reaches me, the willow tree, and stops. The river is still in the dark of night.

Asphodel finishes his chant and falls to his knees, overcome with weakness. He struggles to push himself up onto his hands. He looks at the willow. Even from across the camp, I can feel his confusion. When he sees that I am alone under the willow tree, his eyes fill with anger. He raises a hand and points it at me.

"Seize her!" he yells, though his voice falters as if with old age. "Find the fairy!"

I had hoped to give Bixel more time to get away, but our ruse has been discovered. I jump up, throw the cut chains off me, and run for my life.

The river is too deep and fast for me to cross. I must go along the riverbank until I am outside the sphere of light and make my way around the encampment to the forest. As I charge pell-mell, I am forced to vault over various reeds and sundry shrubberies whilst wearing a giant red velvet dress. Though I am quite fast, I am hindered, and the men-at-arms are closing in on me.

In a moment of hysterical clarity, very similar to the one I experienced whilst chained to the stake and waiting to be eaten by Dragon, I consider that women wear these ridiculous skirts and binding corsets because men find them attractive, but men might only say they find encumbering attire attractive because they make women easier to catch.

I make it out of the sphere of light and scan the ground for any handy rock or sharp stick that I might use to defend myself— but I am taken down by the fastest of my pursuers. I fight, and we tumble across the ground, but he is quickly joined by one of his comrades.

Then, I hear a deafening yet beloved sound.

I lift my head enough to see Dragon. Half his body is still submerged in the water as he pulls his great mass out of the rushing river. He has surfaced beside the willow tree. He sniffs it, and finding it empty, raises his great golden head, and trumpets loudly as if he were trying to shatter our skulls with the sound of his rage.

A moment passes as Dragon scans the enchanted daylight sphere. Soldiers who had been frozen in terror spring to life again, as he looks through them, seeking for me. They have but a breath to run for their lives.

Then he fills his golden belly with air.

Light builds inside of him as he puffs wider and wider. He uproots the willow tree, gouging enormous troughs into the ground as he hauls himself fully onto land. He digs his talons deep into the dark earth and then he breathes out and sets the encampment ablaze.

Men scream. The wooden turrets that would have shot him from the sky flame brightly and tumble to the ground. A river of fire spills from Dragon's jaws, washing over everything in its path— except for one place.

Asphodel, still on his knees, holds up a hand with his palm facing Dragon. His thumb holds down his middle finger, and the other three fingers are raised in a sign of power. Blue light surges out from him and divides the molten wave of Dragon's fire into two channels that flow around Asphodel, leaving him unburnt.

Dragon's breath ends. Asphodel falls flat onto the ground, unconscious, and the sphere of daylight around the camp goes out. The men holding me start to drag me away.

"Dragon!" I scream.

He turns his great head, and his green eyes seem to glow. Though it is completely dark now that Asphodel's enchantment has run out, Dragon sees me. His eyes narrow in anger at the men restraining me, and with a hiss, he lunges across the ground toward us. My captors drop me and run away, screaming in terror.

Dragon's claw snatches me off the ground and lifts me until I am level with his eyes. He makes a grumbly, growling sound.

"I'm all right," I say, reaching out to touch his snout. "I am uninjured," I reiterate. I gesture urgently behind him. "Asphodel—" I say. We both turn to look.

Asphodel is gone.

Dragon huffs smoke and sparks out his nostrils. Then, he

cages me in his claw and vaults into the dark sky. His wings push down, and I am flattened against his talons, looking down at the burning towers, the dead men, and a very stunned Sir Lakely.

I feel Dragon's wingbeats as we climb higher and higher above the madness, and then I float as we soar through the starry, quiet darkness.

19

Dragon lands in the courtyard behind the forge and changes into a man without ever letting me go. Though I feel him shift around me, I can't quite pin my eyes on the transformation. It seems as if one moment I am in Dragon's claw and the next I am in his arms. He places my feet on the ground and holds me so tightly I can feel his heart pounding against my chest. I wrap my arms around his bare back and lean against him.

"He hurt you?" Dragon asks, his face buried in my neck.

"No," I reply.

"So scared," he says.

"Me too." I let go of a breath I didn't realize I had been holding.

"Right, we'll give you a moment, then!" Crat announces loudly.

Dragon and I break apart and he moves behind me, looking for his clothes, while I face the others.

"Crat? When did you get back?" I ask.

"Right about the time you were getting snatched. Bit too late to stop it, though. Sorry," he says apologetically. "I told Lord Dragon what Asphodel had planned by taking you, and what was waiting for him with all those dragon bows. I thought he should wait for dark and use the river."

"Your plan worked," I reply, trying not to sound as surprised as I feel. "Good thinking."

"Not easy to get him to wait, though," Lakonius adds.

"That's a way to put it," Jack remarks, snorting. She gestures to the ground and when I look, I notice there is no longer any grass, just scorched earth.

"He nearly burned the forge down," Putter says, rubbing the back of his neck, laughing nervously.

Dressed now, Dragon takes my hand and pulls me toward the forge. "Inside, Jonara," he says, frowning.

We pass a stump and a pile of wood chips that used to be a tree, I think. "What happened to the tree?" I ask.

"Me waiting," he growls. His eyes flash and I leave it at that.

Jack grabs ahold of my hand when I pass her. I stop and give her a hug. She clings to me with her wiry little arms and says, "Glad you're back," before releasing me and running inside.

"Are you hungry?" Mistress Waverly asks as I enter the forge. She gestures to a table that wasn't in the forge before. On it, food and plates and cups of wine and water are already laid. "I had some food brought over."

I don't feel much like eating yet, but I thank her anyway.

She pulls me into a fierce hug. When she lets me go, she sniffs and turns to surreptitiously wipe her eyes.

"A good meal will steady everyone's nerves. You all should wash your hands before you sit at the table," she says in a scolding tone. "This forge is filthy. Look, I've got soot in my eyes again!"

"Come here, girl," Limond says, pulling her into a hug. "We know it's not the soot, you softie."

Mistress Waverly has had enough of all this nonsense. "She's back now, and unharmed, and we have plenty of work to do," she says, waving Limond away.

The lockboxes demand an inspection before I can sit and eat. "And the lock mechanism?" I ask, feeling the smooth front before putting the key in the keyhole to make sure it turns. "Is it well-covered by dragon scales?"

Ellison nods. "You could drop it off a mountain and it wouldn't break," he assures me, though I'm more worried about Asphodel's spells.

"These are beautifully made, Ellison. Lakonius." I look at them each and smile.

"Nearly done, Lady Jonara," Ellison says proudly. "Just two more to go, and those are well along already."

I nod. "Good. Asphodel is low on funds. He needs Lord Dragon's hoard, or he can't pay his army, which is the main reason he took me." I feel Dragon move even closer to me, although he is already so close he's nearly trod on my foot several times. "And I have more good news. Asphodel no longer has the power to steal names, not without killing himself in the process. When we face him in battle, the only spells he'll be able to cast will be illusion."

"How did you manage that, lass?" Crat asks in disbelief.

"I freed his fairy," I reply, grinning. I tell them about Bixel and how Asphodel used him. Then I turn to Dragon. "Bixel's on his way here. He knows you. He knows your name."

"What?" Dragon says, stunned.

I smile at him. "It's true."

He looks worried. "And w-what you f-feared...?"

I shake my head rather than make him say it, for I know how he dislikes speaking in front of others. "You're not married," I reply quietly.

His smile is hopeful and full of promises. "Yet."

I gaze at him longer than I should, but I don't care. A few hours ago, I didn't know if I'd ever see him again. It's not that he's become more beautiful to me, but my time with him certainly has. So, I don't care if I stare and others see me do it. He's my Dragon now.

"Young love. That's the stuff right there," Crat says, sniffling.

"Is *everyone* going to cry?" Ellison asks.

"I might," Putter says, shrugging. Ellison shoves him with an elbow. "What? It's touching. Now, let's drink some wine and eat some food. We've got our Lady Jonara back, a fine meal, a job well done, and I say that's enough for a celebration!"

"Here, here!" Limond seconds gustily.

I would rather be alone with Dragon to recover from the shock of my abduction, but it seems everyone needs reassurance right now that I am truly returned to them. We sit together at the table and try to get back to normal. We pass around plates of food and bottles of drink while they fill me in on all I've missed. Dragon presses his leg against mine under the table and repeatedly touches me as if to reassure himself that I am there, while Putter informs me of Glomsby's progress. I had received a letter from him in my absence. Dragon wraps his arm around my back as I bend to read it.

Glomsby's letter informs me that he has appointed over twenty recruiters and they have all ridden out to gather forces. He has included a map with rough X's over the towns that have been assigned an enlistment force.

"*Please send funds to the demarcated towns as soon as possible. Best, Glomsby*," I read aloud, finishing the letter. I let out a sigh, staring at the map. "That's a lot of towns," I say.

Dragon shakes his head and points at the map. He circles five towns with his finger and points at the town in the middle of the cluster. "Bank here. Five towns one bank. Ten banks, fifty towns."

"You're right," I say. "If they want to get paid some of them are going to have to travel. But we need to be careful how we choose which towns get the lockboxes."

"Roads," Putter says knowingly. "We need to make sure all these towns have functioning roads between them, so the people can get to and from without being robbed."

His words remind me of something. I take a good look at the map. "I know these roads," I say, frowning. "I've walked them. They're riddled with bandits."

Dragon looks at me sharply and squeezes my arm. "Bandits?" he says quietly, his eyes narrowed.

"I'm scrappier than I look, Dragon," I reply, grinning. "I can handle a ruffian or two, but not everyone can. We must clear the roads between the banks, or we will have no safe way to pay the recruits."

"Or their families," Ellison adds. "That's why young men enlist, yes? To feed their families. Some of the people coming to these banks will be the wives, mothers, and children. Easy pickings for a bandit."

Dragon nods once. "I will clear the roads for the f-families. My job."

We all fall back in silence. A lot of bandits are going to die horrible deaths, and I can tell by the grim look on Dragon's face that he does not relish this thought.

"How about putting the word out that we need men of derring-do?" I suggest. "We'll recruit the bandits first if we can. And if we can't, then the Dragon Lord will do what he must."

"I'll start working the tavern," Limond says. "Most of those lads just need jobs." He raises his cup. "I'd say many will find it preferable to take the Dragon Lord's colors and his coin than to get eaten by him."

"Better pay and much less painful," Lakonius agrees heartily.

Though I know this is how Limond will jovially inspire other men to sign their names on our list of recruits, I also know it bothers Dragon to be spoken of in this way. The thought of eating a person is loathsome to him, and that others believe him capable of it disturbs him deeply. But we must allow it. The specter of his ferocity will serve his ultimate purpose.

We finish our meal with more pleasant conversation and agree to retire early. Tomorrow we plan to finish the final two lockboxes, fill them, and when nightfall comes again Dragon and I will begin flying them out.

I am keenly aware of how impatient Dragon becomes as we take our long leave of the others, and if they notice that we are the first to depart, they make no comment.

Our hands entwined, we make our way back to the inn, stealing glances at each other.

He is not married to another, nor has he left anyone behind, I keep thinking. I can be with him. The thought makes me nervous, but also eager as he is to find privacy.

By the time we're mounting the stairs, he and I are both laughing and nearly running to our room. I've never felt so light inside.

Dragon shuts the door behind us and presses me against it, his body against mine. He touches my face, looking over every detail of my features before he leans his mouth towards mine and pauses as if asking for permission. I tip my mouth the last hair's width to his.

I've been kissed before, though I'd hardly compare those kisses to this. I'm not thinking about where to put my nose or how and when to breathe. I'm not searching in vain to find a rhythm to his tongue and lip movement so that I might meet it rather than work against it. I don't have to tilt my head at some strange angle to achieve a relatively pleasant contact. This kiss just *is*, and I fall into it with no thought.

One of his hands holds the nape of my neck and the other the small of my back. His knee presses between my legs and he effortlessly lifts me up onto his hips, breathing me in, pulling my legs around him.

And then he suddenly stops and sets me down. His forehead rests in the crook of my neck, though the rest of his body moves back from me a step. His hands press, open-palmed, against the wood of the door behind me.

"Wait," he says, but more to himself than to me. He looks up at me and smiles. "Almost like I want to eat you."

We both laugh breathy, weak-kneed laughs. I put my fingers in his hair.

"Please do," I say hazily, as I watch gold dust eddy in the air.

He rubs his jawbone along mine, leaving his perfume. Then he takes my shoulders in his hands, spins me around while he walks me backward, and sits me down on the edge of the bed. He kneels in front of me and removes his shirt.

"When you were taken, a part of my heart turned to stone," he says slowly but clearly, and without stuttering. He puts his thumb and first two fingers against his chest and presses. He keeps pressing until blood wells out and I see his fingertips dig down into his skin.

"Dragon!" I grab his wrist to make him stop but he is so much stronger than me that I doubt he even feels it.

He pulls his fingers out of his chest and holds up a diamond the size of a walnut. He sighs with relief.

"What have you done to yourself?" I ask desperately. I'm on my knees now too, scrabbling for a spare bit of cloth. I tear off a bit of the bedclothes and press it to Dragon's chest. I wipe the blood away and find no wound.

"Hurts more *in* than taking it out," he tells me. "Had to do it."

There were only a few drops of blood, but I keep wiping at the place he pushed his hand in, expecting to find that he's damaged himself in some way, but he hasn't. I sniffle and realize I'm crying.

"Don't you *ever* do that again!" I shout. I throw the cloth at him for good measure.

He smiles at me and catches me in his arms. "Don't ever leave me again."

"I won't!" I holler, mildly hysterical.

"Marry me, Jonara," he says, giving me the diamond.

I look at the piece of his heart in my hand. It's pure as snow and full of fire and stars.

"Yes," I whisper.

I feel his hands tilting my head back and his mouth sweeping across mine. As I pour myself against him, he catches every drop. He lifts me up and lays me on the bed. He grins while he kisses me.

"You'll marry me?" he asks.

"Yes," I repeat, grinning back.

We laugh and kiss and fall on each other as we roll about in the bed. Our play turns serious, and our laughs turn to sighs. Laces are pulled free. Clothes whisper as they fall off the skin. We arch closer to each other to ease the ache that closeness brings, yet Dragon repeatedly stops himself, insisting we wait.

Eventually, we find sleep in sweet torture.

When I wake, I feel Dragon is already stirring behind me and I move against him. He rolls on top of me and holds me still underneath him.

"We marry today," he insists, his eyes bright with need.

"Can we get my Da first?" I ask gingerly. "It might delay things, but it would make him so happy."

Dragon nods and takes a deep breath. "We'll get your father today," he says, his hands smoothing up and down my body. "Must be today," he growls.

Suddenly overcome with a hunger for food instead of just each other, Dragon and I quickly wash and dress. We hurry down to the tavern with our arms entwined.

I'm astonished to see that Bixel is sitting at a table with Glomsby, who has returned to us. With them are Putter, Crat, Ellison, Jack, and Lakonius. Bixel's iridescent wings are on full display as he tells a raucous story that he ends as soon as we enter the tavern.

Bixel's face falls. He gives me one look of regret before he crosses to Dragon, and puts a hand on his shoulder.

"David Allen Waits. My friend. You have ten days to complete your quest. If you do not kill Asphodel in that time, you will die."

20

Dragon—David—stands completely still. He doesn't even breathe. His face drains of color and his eyes stare. Then, he looks over at me.

"Oh no," he says.

He puts both his hands in his hair, squeezing his eyes shut, and utters a word I'm not familiar with, though I can tell it's a curse word by the way he says it. He looks at me again, his face continually changing with too many thoughts and feelings to list, but I can see a difference in him. He doesn't look at me the same way.

He presses a hand to his chest and grimaces like something inside of him hurts. "Oh, Jonara, I'm so sorry."

I shift on my feet, not sure what to ask, or if I want to ask anything at all. I don't think I'd like the answers he'd give me.

"Why don't you meet us at the forge, yeah?" Putter suggests. "Come on, lads. We'll let them work this out."

Everyone but Bixel stands and leaves us, but all I can

really see is the expression on David's face. He looks like he's caught in a trap. The edges of my world seem to darken as if I'm looking at him from the bottom of a deep hole.

"There *is* someone waiting for you," I guess. I gesture with my hand. "Your diamond tooth."

"There's no one for me but you."

"You have a family. Parents. A reason to return," I list, unable to believe him.

"No. I never knew my father and my mother died a year before I came here. I had friends, of course, but no one who needs me. I've broken no heart, but my own. I made my diamond tooth when I failed the last time I challenged Asphodel." David looks at Bixel, momentarily relieved. "I thought you had died before he took my name."

"I mean, I was *mostly* dead, but I'm quite better now," Bixel replies.

"I'm glad you made it out."

"Jonara saved me, you know."

David looks at me and smiles. "She saved both of us, then." Then he swallows hard. "I can't do this to her," he says, looking back at Bixel.

"Do what?" I ask. But David won't answer me. I look at Bixel. "Do what?" I demand.

"David said a spell to bring him here on the condition that he had one year to kill Asphodel, and if he didn't, he'd die. His year is up in ten days." Bixel replies, looking uncharacteristically serious.

"Okay," I say, nodding. "I spent a long time on the road with my father. This isn't the first time I've encountered a knight on a quest, you know." I turn to David. "This is a difficult situation, but you're not going to die. I know you will kill Asphodel."

His face falls. "But *if* I complete my quest, I go back. I'm out of Lucitopia forever."

"Lucitopia?" I repeat, frowning in thought.

"Can she come back with me?" David asks Bixel, hopefully.

Bixel shakes his head. "In your world, she's just a dream." Then he gets an idea. "You *could* tell her, about... you know. But then you'd definitely be stuck here."

"I don't care. I *want* to stay," David insists. His face twists. "But what would it do to her, to learn that she's...?"

"It's an existential crisis of the highest order," Bixel concludes, shrugging. "I doubt I could do it to someone I hated, much less someone I loved."

I look between the two friends suspiciously. "What's this about me being a dream? And what's an existential crisis?"

"Nothing!" Bixel gives me a dashing smile. He waves a hand in the air in a fluttery motion. "You are David's dream girl, is all I meant."

"Oh," I say, startled by the compliment.

But was that really what he meant? There seems to be a lot of glitter in the air, and it's distracting me. For a moment, it seemed like they were talking about... I'm not sure any more.

Glitter. Like a fairy did a magic spell.

"Bixel, did you just put an enchantment on me?" I ask, incredulous.

"A very mild one. Honestly, it's for your own good," he says as if I'm complaining like some fussy babe. Bixel turns to

David. "I'm sorry for both of you, but we don't have much time. You're a right pain in my glitter-maker, David Allen Waits, but I've grown rather fond of you. I'd be upset if you died."

Bixel squeezes my arm and puts something in my hand. It's Dragonbarb. He gives me a brave smile on his way out the door.

David and I stare at each other for far too long. Neither of us knows how to begin to end it.

"I'm so sorry," he says quietly.

I nod. "You've said that already." We stare at each other some more while it sinks in. "When you leave, you're never coming back, are you?"

He swallows hard and shakes his head. "I know it's the worst thing I could do to you."

"Not really," I say. "But close." I try to laugh, but it doesn't sound right. "At least you've given me a warning. It's not like you'll just disappear one day without any explanation, like my parents. Though you haven't really explained anything to me, have you?"

"I can't," he says helplessly. "Believe me, Jonara. None of this changes the way I feel about you."

He reaches for me, but I evade his hands. "Don't think I blame you," I say, my voice unnaturally loud, like it doesn't belong to me. "I'm not angry. You didn't know. How could you know? You could barely remember how to speak, though I notice you don't have problems now."

He stops trying to hold me and stands with his arms at his sides in a posture that's as unnatural to him as my voice has become to me. Neither of us is acting like ourselves.

We've given too much of ourselves to the other to know what comes naturally to us any more.

"Do you want to know the strangest thing?" he asks. I nod. "The strangest thing is now that I remember who I was before, I love you even more."

Shock was holding me together, but now that it's passing, I think I might come apart. I turn and run from the tavern, but David catches me just outside the door.

"Please let me go," I beg.

"No," he replies, though it hurts him to see me struggle, albeit uselessly. He's so much stronger than I am that I can't even budge one finger on his hand no matter how I twist.

"Dragon—"

"David," he corrects softly.

"David," I say, though I swallow half of his name in a sob. "You've taken all my other feelings. At least let me have my sadness."

He makes a broken sound, but still, he shakes his head. "I'll let you go, but I can't let you out of my sight. The last time I did that you got taken," he says, then he releases me.

I run, but I hear his wings above me. He's flying in daylight. While I don't see any dragon bows set up in the middle of the street, it's still dangerous for him. I stop and turn to face him.

"Are you trying to get yourself killed?" I yell at him as he lands. He's in the form of a man with dragon wings, holding his shirt in his hand.

He touches his chest and rounds his shoulders, nearly doubling over with a pained expression on his face. "Maybe?" he answers uncertainly.

"Well, stop it," I say, wiping at my eyes. I turn and walk away from him. He follows me, of course. I wheel around again. "You're not even going to give me one second alone?"

He shakes his head, pressing against his chest in obvious physical pain.

"What's wrong?" I ask. Then I remember the diamond he gave me, and how it was made. I take it out of my pocket. "If you're making another of these, you may keep them both."

I hold it out for him, but he won't take it.

"I can't keep it, or Dragonbarb," I tell him, adding the precious blade to the parts of him I wish to give back. "Take them back. I don't want them."

"Then throw them in the street," he replies harshly, bent over in pain.

I almost do. Yet, though I tell my hands to open and let these pieces of him go, my hands will not obey. I put the diamond in one pocket, Dragonbarb in the other, and stomp toward the forge.

At least I'm angry now and not just sad. I'm angry because I'm worried about him. How dare he make me think more of him than of myself at this particular moment? This is *my* heartbreak. *My* abandonment. I should at least be able to think of my pain over someone else's for once, yet I can't because I can't stop worrying about *bloody* Dragon. I mean David. Bloody David.

That blasted monster.

I can hear him wheezing behind me. By the time we get to the forge, I can't even pretend to be angry with him any more.

"Come here," I tell him, putting one of his arms over my shoulders. His knees buckle and I'm forced to nearly carry him into the forge.

The sounds of hammers ringing, bellows being pumped, and fires roaring seem to pause as soon as our friends see us.

"Well, that's it, lads. She's up and killed him," Crat says regretfully.

"I didn't—" I begin but decide against explaining. "Jack, clear off the bench."

She hurries to clear a spot, so I may lay David down. He sits but refuses to lie flat, though I try to push him back.

"No," he says, holding my hands away. He exhales sharply, and blood comes spilling out between his lips.

"Jack. Get some wet clothes," I order calmly, though I feel anything but. I want to get her away from the sight of blood. I catch David's head in my hands as it falls forward. I hold his head up and put my face close to his. "It's going to be okay. Whatever it is— just take it out," I tell him gently.

"It's not done... growing yet," he groans. "I need to be bigger." He stands and staggers to the back door of the forge, already pulling at the laces of his breeches.

I run to him and help him through the door. "Here. Let me," I say. I take off his boots because it seems like he's trying to keep his torso extended as long as possible. Whatever it is that's growing inside him has become so large he can barely take a breath around it.

As soon as he's naked I step back so he may transform. He touches my face. "It will be easier when I'm Dragon," he says, groaning with pain, but trying to sound optimistic. "I'll barely feel it then."

"Okay," I say, nodding. Urging him to change. "Go on then."

"I love you," he says.

"Obviously," I reply, rolling my eyes. Before I'm done speaking, he has changed. "Impossible beast."

He makes a rumbling sound like he's laughing, but I can't laugh with him. Even in his draconian form, he looks ill. He is not golden any more. Over most of his body, he is the dun color of old straw, and his burnished wings have turned muddy beige. His paler underbelly has drained of nearly all color, leaving it ashy white.

I reach up and touch his snout. It feels lukewarm at best, and his scent is barely there. When I remove my hand there is no gold dust on my fingers.

"Oh, Dragon," I sigh. "What's happened to you?"

He makes his mewling noise and huffs cool air around me. He lays his head down on his claws. His big emerald eyes seem dark.

There are rules to the spell Dragon is under, and yet I can't help him because they are hidden from me. I'm suddenly angry again, but not at him.

"Bixel!" I shout, turning away from Dragon and marching into the forge.

"Yes, Lady Jonara?" he asks warily.

"You understand this magic spell David has undertaken, don't you?"

"Some of it. My quest was to aid David in killing Asphodel, but I wound up getting captured and making Asphodel a hundred times stronger." Bixel gives me a sobering look. "So, that should give some indication as to how much I know about all this."

"What's happening to David?"

"I don't know," Bixel replies seriously. "But I don't think we have much time."

"Why is that?" I ask, stepping closer to him. "Is there another condition to the spell you haven't yet told me?"

He takes a step back, eyeing me fearfully. "You know dragon blood is quite powerful, and you're covered in it?"

I raise an eyebrow at him. "If you don't want fairy blood joining it, I suggest you answer me. What's growing inside of David and how do I get it out?"

"I don't know," he repeats gently. He frowns in thought. "I'm worried about him too, Jonara. I'm not familiar with the inner workings of a Dragon Lord's anatomy, though I do know that one of the few ways to kill a dragon... is to break its heart."

21

I pace about the forge for a solid quarter of an hour. My companions are huddled in a tight group, conferring amongst themselves. All but Jack. She has quietly tucked herself into a small corner to file a small bit of metal that only I know is the skeleton key.

"Glomsby," I call out when I feel like I have a handle on things again.

"Yes, milady?" he replies, breaking himself away from a heated exchange with Crat.

"Where are those men you promised me?"

"Camped outside of town, milady. I did not want to bring so many armed men into such a small hamlet," he says thoughtfully. "Mistress Waverly is with them, making sure they are supplied."

"Excellent," I respond. "Lakonius. Ellison. Are all of the lockboxes finished?"

"Yes, milady," Ellison answers. "Our work now is to make as many arms as we are able."

"Good. We shall fill the lockboxes and send them out immediately," I say as I retrieve a parchment and pencil to write down an account of it all.

"Are you sure about that?" Crat asks. "I mean, considering?" He points toward the back where Dragon is resting and raises a doubtful eyebrow.

"The plan hasn't changed," I announce. I go to the first lockbox, open it, then cross to one of the bags of gold. "Lord Dragon will meet Asphodel in battle, and he will kill him."

The bright, methodical sound of gold coin dropping into a pile in the lockbox fills the forge as I count.

"And what if he dies before the battle?" Bixel asks gently.

"He won't," I reply.

"Yeah, but what if he does?" Crat says.

"Then I shall take his bones and kill Asphodel myself!" I shout, rounding on Crat. "Was that not your first plan? To kill the dragon and take his bones? Well, if Lord Dragon dies, he will have saved you that first step." I turn about the room, meeting each gaze with my own. "You all think we've been defeated, but we've never been closer to victory. The last I saw of Asphodel he had worked a spell, thinking he could draw power from Bixel, but Bixel had already been freed. Doing real magic without a fairy powering him nearly killed Asphodel, and for all we know he's in worse shape than David is right now. We must move forward with our plan, *now* while Asphodel is weak." I end on Glomsby. "Can I still count on you and your men, or am I to do all this alone?"

"Milady," Glomsby says, bowing deeply, and then

standing straight again to address me. "As you said, my intent was to take the dragon bones and face Asphodel myself, with no Dragon Lord to lead me and no army to follow me. My resolve is as it always was."

"Take a knee," I tell him solemnly. Glomsby kneels. "In the name of the Dragon Lord, I grant you knighthood. You shall ride out in front of his army bearing his banner, which shall be a golden dragon on a red field. Have the banner made and appoint your own banner man. I shall supply your armor. It will be made with dragon scales."

I look over at Lakonius and Ellison to find their faces already screwed up with thought and excitement as they start to imagine how to go about making this armor.

"Thank you, my Lady," Sir Glomsby says, bowing his head, his voice rough with emotion.

"Rise, good Sir Knight." I smile at him and go back to counting the gold. "I need you to supply me with ten men per box. Each box will need to travel in a fortified carriage, with a team of six horses. Ten by ten men with arms and armor, and ten by six horses with drivers and carriages. Can you supply all this if I give you the gold to acquire it?"

"I can and will, milady," he replies. He bows again before departing.

"Bixel," I call out, my eyes still on my task. "What kind of magic can you do?"

"Ah— fairy magic?" he says, uncertain how to answer me.

"Can you enchant the carts and the armed guards to make them invisible?" I say, clarifying my intent. "Or can you make them appear to be a group of traveling minstrels?"

"That's good thinking," Bixel says, looking pleasantly surprised. "The second option would be preferable because I wouldn't have to also make all the dust invisible and the sound disappear— invisibility is quite hard actually," he adds for my edification.

I make a mark in my book and keep counting. "And will you have to travel with the carts?" I ask Bixel.

"Yes— well, no. A *fairy* must go with each, but I have friends." Bixel smiles.

"How soon can they get here?"

Bixel shrugs. "I'll fly now and see how many I can get."

"Do the very best you can."

"Yes, milady," Bixel says. I can hear the smile in his speech, though I am presently too occupied to see it.

"Crat," I say loudly before he can sneak off in Bixel's wake. "I have a job for you, too."

"Yes? Er— milady," he adds hastily.

"There is a Sir Lakely serving Asphodel."

"I know of him," Crat replies.

"I got the distinct impression that he was beginning to doubt his allegiance." I pause and look up at Crat. "Is there any way you can gain access to him and offer him a place with Lord Dragon?"

Crat narrows his eyes at me. "Trying to steal Asphodel's best general, then? You're a right terror, you are," he says appreciatively. "I'll see what I can do."

After Crat has left, Ellison walks past me, wiping down his tools and chuckling to himself. "Keeping everyone busy, so they can't get cold feet?" he asks.

"I'm keeping everyone focused on our goal," I reply, but I

glance up at Ellison with a knowing smile. "And moving feet are less likely to get cold than still ones," I admit.

Ellison smiles but does not raise any objections. Neither does Lakonius. In fact, they both seem revived to their task and immediately begin discussing how to fit dragon scales inside the armor.

I spend the rest of the morning filling the lockboxes and accounting for each piece of gold in Dragon's hoard, whilst deciding which towns will receive how much. I allot a large portion of coin to the bills I must settle here in town, then I lock the boxes and hang every key— save the skeleton key currently in Jack's possession— on a metal ring. I hook the keychain onto my belt and sling a fat purse over my shoulder that jingles with the gold I need to settle some debts this day.

Then I go outside to see Dragon. I run my hand over his hide, and he sighs. He feels cold. "It's all right, Dragon," I whisper. When I look up at him his eyes have opened to slits which he lets slide closed.

I stride back inside and announce, "I leave to seek Mistress Waverly in the encampment outside of town."

"Shouldn't you be wanting some kind of guard with you, milady?" Lakonius asks, gesturing to the keys and the fat coin purse about my person.

"He's quite right. I will escort you as soon as I see the carriage loaded," Glomsby says from the door. He has rejoined us after securing my demands and now waits upon me. An odd thought, that. To know I have attendants.

"My thanks, good Sir Knight." I join him at the door. Outside the forge are the armored carriages and guards I asked for.

I watch as the men work in teams to haul the heavy lockboxes out of the forge and into their respective carriages. Meanwhile, I hope that Bixel will return soon with his fairy friends. If he doesn't, I'll just have to pray that the dangerous-looking men, bristling with arms, that Glomsby has assembled are the only deterrent needed to get the gold safely to their appointed towns.

I give the drivers instructions as to which town they are to deliver their precious cargo as I pass the respective key to Sir Glomsby. Each key-bearer seems to be a friend of his, and he embraces each and wishes them luck in turn. Along with their key, he gives each one my detailed list of instructions for how the gold is to be spent, and what the exchange rate will be with other non-dragon coins.

While we go through this process and I answer any remaining questions the new bankers have, we wait on Bixel. When there is nothing left for me to explain, we pass nervous glances around like a serving tray.

"Where is he?" I mutter.

"He probably stopped to have lunch," Jack says brightly, breaking the tension.

Sir Glomsby's eyes meet mine, and we share a look of resignation. We both know this gold must be en route today. We nearly call it— when Bixel plummets to the earth and lands between us, still holding a bottle of a bilious-colored spirit.

"Sorry, sorry," Bixel says, waving his arms and sloshing alcohol this way and that.

"You're drunk," Jack says, surprised.

"I am, young Jack," Bixel replies, squinting down at her.

"I lost a bet to my stupid brother." He tumbles over onto Sir Glomsby, who rights him again. "You're a handsome one, aren't you?" Bixel notices. He squeezes Sir Glomsby's bicep and makes an appreciative sound.

"Bixel," I say, stepping forward to peel him off Sir Glomsby. "Where are your friends?"

"What?" he replies, confused.

I sigh and try not to lose my patience. "The friends you promised? The fairies who were going to enchant the carriages?"

Bixel waves his arms about, laughing. "Oh, they're not friends, really. More like subjects." He tilts his head back and sings a few notes in a surprisingly melodious voice.

Ten fairies, of every hue in the rainbow, and with shimmering, iridescent wings, appear in the air and descend. They drop in a perfect circle around the inebriated Bixel and take a knee, bowing down to him.

"We are at your command, Prince Bixel," the red fairy says in a chiming voice. She seems to be the leader.

"Prince?" Jack shouts in astonishment. "You're fairy royalty? High Court?"

Bixel rolls his eyes. "My parents are the king and queen, but they had twenty-one children, dear Jack. I'm not going to inherit or anything, so don't get in a—" he hiccups loudly, "tizzy. Rise, my littlings." The rainbow-hued fairies stand around him, keeping their gaze down. "You know the plan. Pick a carriage and cast your enchantments. You all get goodies if you are... er... good."

Bixel dissolves into a giggling mess and tips over onto Sir Glomsby again.

"I believe the cargo should be sent on its way, milady," Sir Glomsby says as he tries to keep Bixel upright.

I turn to the carriages. "Ride fast. Keep each other safe. And thank you for your bravery."

The men bow to me as one, some of them murmuring, *Thank you, Lady Jonara*. Then, they climb up and the carriages pull away in a storm of hooves and dust.

"You remind me of my mum," Bixel tells me. "Except you're not two thousand years old... are you?" He bursts into laughter and dissolves against Sir Glomsby.

"I'll take him out back and return to escort you to Mistress Waverly at the camp, milady," the good knight tells me. When Sir Glomsby returns to me, he's blushing.

"What happened?" I ask.

"I left Prince Bixel under Lord Dragon's talons. That should sober him up."

"That wasn't what I meant," I reply with a raised eyebrow. "There's glitter on your lips." I search Sir Glomsby's face, but his blush only deepens, and he does not offer up any more information.

We hasten through the town toward the encampment in silence before he speaks. "From this point on I believe you should always have an escort, milady. I will appoint Putter to the task."

I know he's right, though it chafes at me. "There will be no need presently," I say crisply. "Lord Dragon will soon be well enough to watch over me."

I hear Glomsby's breath of laughter and turn to see him smiling at me, shaking his head.

"You don't think he'll survive?" I challenge.

"I do not fear for his life."

"You don't?"

"Milady, the only thing that would make me afraid for him would be if he were to disobey you."

I smile at his convivial teasing but must look down lest he ferret out the worry behind the mirth in my eyes.

"He will recover. He's had a shock, is all," Glomsby says quietly, marking my fear despite my attempts to hide it behind bluster. "I know what it is to wake one day and find the world turned over and falling down around you, as he has. He will recover."

I've already asked him to pledge his life to my cause. Though it is forward of me, I may as well ask him the reason he's willing to give it so readily.

"What happened to you?" I ask.

Glomsby is silent for a long time, though I know it is only to gather his thoughts, and not to refuse answering my question. I walk quietly beside him, watching the light play across his dark skin.

"I was born in a small village. I was always the fastest, strongest, and smartest. I was better with bow and arrow, sword and staff," he says, sounding disdainful of these blessings. "Everyone encouraged me to leave. Go, seek my fortune in the south, as all promising young men are told to do. In my absence, Asphodel came. By the time I returned to my village, full of ordinary people who told me I was too good to remain among them, they'd all starved to death." His eyes sparkle with tears. "Men, women, children. All of them. They'd forgotten to eat."

I swallow, but my voice is still hoarse when I speak. "I'm so sorry."

"I can't even remember my mother's name. I didn't have it written down when he stole it," he says, sounding like his thoughts are far away.

I don't know how to comfort him, so I don't try. Instead, I wait for him to talk, or not talk as he sees fit.

Eventually, Sir Glomsby clears his throat and says, "They say Asphodel conquers without violence, but it's not without cost. And he must pay."

We have reached the encampment. We pause before entering and I turn to face him. "Take heart, good Sir Glomsby. I'm a bullish accountant," I tell him. He smiles sadly at me, and I clasp his hand in mine until the warmth of his smile finally reaches his eyes. "I promise you. Asphodel will pay all he owes."

22

We enter the encampment and I find Mistress Waverly atop a farmer's cart, directing the distribution of the produce to a series of runners. Putter is here. He has a team of burly men around him, all of them guarding the provisions coming off the cart.

When Mistress Waverly sees me, she delegates her task to someone else and jumps down. She greets me with a warm embrace and notices the enormous coin purse slung across my body.

"Oh good! You brought some gold," she says, relieved, and starts in on a seemingly endless list of debts that need paying.

The rest of my afternoon is spent seeing to the most pressing issues of the camp— which are blankets, boots, and of course, food. I'm fast learning that armies are full of young men who go through boots almost as quickly as they go through food— though there really is nothing they go through faster than food. The sooner we go to battle, the fewer days we'll need to feed them.

What's more, a lot of these men, I see, are not much more than ruffians dressed in rags. The plan to recruit the bandits rather than kill them is working quite well, and though they are only just beginning to trickle in from the surrounding towns and countryside, they come supplied with their own weapons. However, they require almost all other provisions and clothes to get them up to fighting form. Tunics. Cloaks. And of course, boots. These we must secure before the trickle becomes a flood, and a flood it will be shortly.

When I first planned this war, I thought making weapons would take the longest and require the most money. I couldn't have been more wrong. The countryside has been arming itself for the past year, but it has not been clothing itself. Or bathing itself, much to my dismay. It seems the entire kingdom has been poised on a precipice, and at the slightest word they have been prepared to drop everything and come at Dragon's call, like the last few chapters of a storybook when months of preparation pass in a few quick sentences.

Putter looms over us protectively, scratching his bushy beard and harrumphing, as Mistress Waverly and I tackle the financial complexities of supply and demand. We take our lunch there, out in the open with the men, sharing in the simple but fortifying rations that we expect them to eat. Barley and mutton stew. Hearty black bread and a bit of cheese or butter. A few mouthfuls of pickled cabbage here or there.

Afterward, Sir Glomsby goes out among them to gather information on the new recruits. On the rare occasion that I lift my head from the stack of bills I must sort through and pay, I notice that more than a few of the new men are wearing Asphodel's colors. They are deserters. Knowing that heartens me.

I'm happy for the work. The never-ending problems of others keep me from falling down the steep staircase of my own, and my worries for David fade behind the rows of sums that need tallying... though they never disappear. It seems a thousand times I stamp his seal— the silhouette of a dragon in red ink that I invented— into some missive or another. A thousand times more I invoke his name, granting myself power as the proxy of Lord Dragon. I try to be my best self, and I hope that's good enough in his stead.

The sun finally sets and Sir Glomsby, Putter, Mistress Waverly, and I leave the camp and head back to town for our supper. Rather than think about David, I begin to build a timetable in my head. The gold is out. The men are assembling much more quickly than I had thought plausible. The clock is ticking. The only thing left to decide is when and where this battle will take place.

"Sir Glomsby. Do you have any idea where Asphodel is now?" I ask.

"Apparently, he's moved his army to the Forest of Woe," Glomsby replies.

"The Forest of Woe," Mistress Waverly repeats, dumbfounded. "Why? There are monsters there at every turn. That will decimate his numbers."

"We don't know why. We only know what a few deserters

have told us," Glomsby says with a worried frown. "Asphodel was near death, having unwittingly performed a spell without access to fairy magic— as you yourself described, milady. Nonetheless, he had himself tied to his horse when several attempts proved that he was too weak to stay in the saddle. Then he gave the order for his army to ride into the Forest of Woe. That was when many of his soldiers deserted him and came to us."

We walk in silence as we contemplate such a baffling choice.

"We must move south to meet him, then," I say finally. "We must get there before he exits the forest."

"You don't plan on going *in* there do you?" Mistress Waverly asks, shocked.

"Of course not!" I exclaim, horrified by the very thought.

"Well, you did take up with a *dragon*, milady, which is technically a monster," Putter argues as delicately as he can.

"It's entirely different," I rebut, offended. "Dragons are great and terrible, yes, but they are also magnificent. There are some truly gruesome things in the Forest of Woe— things I have no wish to encounter."

"We were just making sure," Mistress Waverly says, leveling Putter with a scolding look. "No offense meant to Lord Dragon."

"We wait for Asphodel *outside* the Forest of Woe," I state bluntly to remove any remaining doubt from their minds.

"If we get there in time, he will be pinned down," Glomsby notes. Then he makes a vexed sound. "Why would he do it? Why would he go into the Forest of Woe? Asphodel's smart. As big as the risk is, there must be an even greater gain, yet I can't fathom it."

I nod, but as we enter the forge, I find I have no answer for him. We are greeted, or rather moved aside, by Lakonius and Ellison who are eager for Sir Glomsby's measurements. They have a helmet and breastplate already fashioned for him but know not the length of his arms and legs.

Jack rushes forward with a stool for Sir Glomsby to stand on. She's got a pencil stuck behind her ear and a roll of parchment in her back pocket, ready to take his measurements. As she passes me, she touches a new chain about her neck, alerting to me its presence. Hidden under her jerkin is the skeleton key I bade her make and keep safe. I give her a secret smile, which she returns before giving her full attention to Sir Glomsby's fitting.

She's still dressed as a boy, which I understand. While Jack need no longer fear being thrown to a dragon, there are thousands of soldiers descending upon this area— far worse in my opinion. I can't fault her father for keeping her sex a secret for a bit longer, though I hope he intends to free her from this deception soon. *If* that is what she wishes, I now consider. Men's clothes do seem to be quite comfortable, and much less prone to singe near to the fire of the forge. Huh. Maybe I'll start wearing breeches when I go back to working my craft after David leaves.

Bixel lies on top of the workbench, moaning softly.

"You can't still be drunk," I say, peering down at him.

"It appears I'm moving past drunkenness and toward regret," he groans.

"How do you feel?" I ask him.

"Like killing my brother," he replies.

"I suppose your parents would be cross if you killed a sibling," I agree.

"Not really. No one likes my brother," Bixel says. "But I can't kill him because he's too bloody powerful."

"You must arise, Prince Bixel," Mistress Waverly informs him. "We're about to eat our supper."

"Just push me onto the floor," Bixel groans. "If I expire whilst you sup, use my corpse as a footrest."

Mistress Waverly and I share a grin.

"I'm going out back," I tell her.

"You should eat something first," she suggests, worried.

"I'm not hungry," I say, crossing the forge to Dragon's courtyard without delay. A few hours and I miss him horribly.

When I get outside, I see he's turned around. His tail faces the door, and his head is toward the river. What a change a few hours have made. No longer pale and dun-colored, Dragon has turned a fiery red that I can make out even in the moonlight. I feel the heat of him from paces away. It's like standing in front of the forge. The ground underneath him is white ash over black-burnt ground. Even the pile of wood chips he whittled in frustration has been reduced to charcoal.

Dragon burns.

"David?" I say as I step around his tail.

He makes a low, growling sound deep in his chest. It sets the ground to rumbling under my feet as I walk around his colossal body toward his great head. He lifts his chin and repositions it on top of his foreclaws so he can look at me.

His eyes are completely black, darker than pitch, with ovals of silver moonlight skimming off the surface of them.

I pull back, alarmed.

"Dragon?" I ask, worried he's no longer there behind those blank button eyes.

He makes a sing-song sound and tilts his head. He stretches his snout toward the river, and I see that he's walled off a semi-circular bath made of rocks at the edge for me. Just like in his cave. He dips his snout into the bath and breathes fire into it. Then, he raises his head and drags his claws under his body weight, painfully hauling himself up.

"No, don't move," I protest, but uselessly.

He turns away for a moment, and then swings his head back, repositioning himself right over the bath. He then opens his jaws and drops a myriad of flowers into the hot water.

The bright perfume of flower petals, coupled with the spice of him, wells up on a hot plume of steam like a blessed cloud. Then Dragon drops his exhausted head back down on his front claws. My face twists with the sudden urge to cry. Always, he thinks of my comfort. Even when he's in pain.

"Thank you," I say. I won't cry. He doesn't need to see me cry any more. Instead, I smile at him and start unlacing my dress. "Won't you come in with me?" I ask saucily.

Dragon tips his snout beneath the water and blows bubbles. I laugh and shuck off my dress as fast as I can. The water is exceptionally hot, and I cringe as I push myself into it. I go to the rock wall that partitions off my bath from the river and remove the top layer of rocks so cooler water can come in, and then I float back to Dragon's snout. Even under water, I can feel the blazing heat of his skin.

Like any fire, he will eventually burn up all his fuel if he doesn't cool down.

"Dragon— or David. Can't tell which you prefer," I say, narrowing my eyes at him.

He makes an indecisive sound, which is as I expected. He likes both, depending on what form he's taken.

"I'll call you Dragon when you're Dragon and David when you're David then," I decide.

He makes a definitive sound.

I continue. "I've decided there's no reason for your heart to be broken," I announce cheerfully. His sparkling black eyes round in question. "It's true," I say, grinning. "You can't have a broken heart if the one you love loves you back with all her heart. And I do. I love you with all my heart, and I will never stop loving you for as long as you live— no matter where that is. And that's a wonderful thing."

Dragon grouses and tries to pull his snout out of the water, but I reach out and hold it. Though he could throw my whole body into the sky without blinking, the simple act of me touching him is enough to restrain him as if I were a team of twenty wild horses. He respects my will as if it were a strength equal to his own. Maybe it is.

"It's all right if you leave me," I tell him, still holding his burning scales in my hands. "I will miss you. It will hurt. But I will go on loving you, and my heart will be whole. And so should yours," I say, pulling his gaze back to mine as he grumbles and looks away.

Dragon makes his mewling sound, and it pulses through the water longingly.

"I wish you could be with me every day so I can love you in person, but second to that is knowing I have tens of thousands of days where I get to love you from afar." I regard him sternly. "But you must *live* for me to love you for the rest of your life. I will not die if you leave me. But if you die, it just might kill me."

He huffs and grumbles, caught in an impossible position. I spin onto my back in the water until I am floating over his nose. We stay like that, staring up at the stars.

23

"Milady," Mistress Waverly calls from the riverbank. I awake and slide off Dragon's nose.

"Yes?" I prompt as I swim to the edge of the pool.

"Crat has returned with Sir Lakely," Mistress Waverly answers. She holds out a towel for me as I climb out of the water.

"He was successful?" I ask, not fully believing it. I dry myself off hastily.

"Hard to say," Mistress Waverly replies. She holds up a fresh dress for me to step into. "He'll speak to none but you."

I braid my hair as she tightens my laces. Between the two of us, we get me dressed and somewhat presentable in a trice.

"I'll be back soon," I whisper to Dragon, running my hand along his hot hide as I stride inside.

The banked fires of the forge cast a small pane of light across the center of the room, illuminating Sir Lakely. He sits in a tall-backed chair, and another has been placed opposite him, with nothing between. In the shadows that twin with the soot-blackened walls, the rest of my friends, and a few of Sir Lakely's bannermen, stand at attention.

The good knight wears his full armor. His hand rests on the pommel of the greatsword which is buckled around his waist. He must sit poker-straight and tilted sideways in his chair to accommodate the greatsword. It rests tip-point on the floor, and the blade is so long that the pommel holds his hand nearly level with his shoulders.

I pause before taking my seat. "What mean you to do with that blade?" I ask, seeing as how its size, positioning, and the firelight that glows upon it have made its mention unavoidable.

"I plan to neither kill nor swear upon it," he says bluntly. "I come in my colors so all may see and know me." He smirks derisively, as if betrayal were more honorable done openly.

I take the seat opposite him. "Though I scarcely know you, I do not think you are a dishonorable man. Lord Dragon is in need of men like you."

The proud bearing of his body changes not at all, but his gaze falters and he looks away uncertainly. "I do not come to join your Dragon Lord. I come to warn him."

"Of what? Another one of Asphodel's traps in the Forest of Woe?"

Sir Lakely shakes his head. "It's not a trap— not exactly."

He pauses, as he searches for the words. "I know little of magic. It is difficult for me to describe what Asphodel has done, and yet disturbing enough that I feel I must part ways with him, though it cost me my life and my honor."

I share a glance with Sir Glomsby before I am forced to

urge Sir Lakely into speaking more. I find I do not want to. "Please, do your best to describe what you have seen, good sir."

He takes a deep breath before beginning. "Upon entering the Forest of Woe, it was clear to me that Lord Asphodel was searching for something— something he needed desperately. I thought it would be a magical talisman, or possibly a well-spring by which to heal himself after your trick with the fairy."

He pauses to smile at me as if to doff his hat at my cleverness, though frankly, it was by luck alone, not artful planning on my part, that Asphodel half-killed himself doing real magic.

"When we came upon the nest of ogres, I thought it was due to the basic circumstances of being in the Forest of Woe, but no. It was the ogres Lord Asphodel wanted." Sir Lakely stops and swallows hard before continuing. "He took them and drained them of their magic, leaving them dead, and himself revived. Enlarged, even, and a bit green in his complexion. Next came the trolls. He muttered his strange words and drew signs in the air. They cracked like rock struck upon a seam and died, and he grew larger still, and glistened like a boulder flecked with crystal."

Sir Lakely's proud bearing falters and he seems to shrink a little.

"I'd seen him take the fairy magic without killing. It was like he was breathing in light and rainbows. But ogre and troll magic are not the same. And the way he takes all they have until they die is not the same." His eyes find mine, and I shiver at what I see in them. "Lord Asphodel is not a man any more. I'm not sure what he's made of himself, but whatever it is it has the power of ten trolls, five ogres, and anything else he's absorbed since I left his company."

"That is... distressing," I say. I glance toward the back doorway. The small gesture is enough to betray my fears to my companions, if not to Sir Lakely. "Yet Asphodel is still no match for a Dragon Lord," I say for everyone's benefit.

"I truly hope so." Sir Lakely stands and bows to me with solemn elegance. "Good luck, Lady Jonara. And goodbye."

"Wait— good Sir Lakely. Where are you going?" I stand hastily. He is already making his way to the door.

"Back to my Lord Asphodel," Sir Lakely replies darkly.

"But he'll kill you!" I exclaim.

"As is his right," Sir Lakely replies. He stops and turns to face me. "I pledged him my life. It is his to take."

What an idiot.

"I'm sorry, Sir Lakely. I can't let you do that." I gesture with my chin and Sir Glomsby shuts the door to the forge.

"What is the meaning of this?" Sir Lakely asks. He's about to start thundering at me, so I wave him off and speak over him.

"I can't let you go off and die an honorable death. I'm sorry— I'm sure you've earned it— but there just aren't enough people who know how to get things done *left* in the world, now that Asphodel has stolen everyone's names."

"Open that door this instant!" Sir Lakely demands, mustache a-quiver. His guards draw their swords. Bixel moves closer to Sir Glomsby by the door, both of them at the ready.

"Stand down everyone," I tell them before continuing.

"One puff and my Lord Dragon could incinerate your entire retinue, Sir Lakely." I gesture out the back door. They see Dragon's black eye filling the doorway, glinting like cold onyx in the moonlight. "What? Did you think he wasn't listening?"

Every arm holding a sword seems to lose its strength at the sight of Dragon. The weapons fall to the floor with a clang. I turn to Sir Lakely.

"I can't let you go. We just don't have the luxury of letting a good knight die a senseless death because he's embarrassed that he backed the wrong man." I hold up a hand before the poor man can get a word out. "Look, I met Asphodel, I understand why you followed him. That's over and done with. Now *we* need you, Sir Lakely." I hold him with my gaze. "You've got to get on with it because we can't let Asphodel win, can we?"

He looks troubled. "That's why I told you what he's becoming. I've done what I can to stop him."

"No, you haven't," I say plainly. "You'd rather die than live dishonored, and while I appreciate your noble sensibilities, I don't have time for them. I've got a war to fight, and I can't spare a single man. I certainly can't spare you. Pull yourself together, all right?" I finish gently because I don't mean to make the man cry. But he does anyway.

Sir Lakely drops his head and his shoulders heave with a sob.

"You didn't have to go *that* far," Putter chides.

I look at him in the shadows. "I was trying to be nice!"

"There's nothing worse than a woman being nice while

she's giving you a tongue-whipping," Lakonius informs me. A thought occurs to him. "Like our mums, really."

I turn back to Sir Lakely. He's already stiffened his upper lip and lifted his head, though his eyes are still red and running.

"I deserve to die, milady," he says. He wipes his eyes and throws his shoulders back. "But before I do, I will try to right some of my wrongs."

"Good," I say, dubiously. I'm not quite sure I agree with his self-imposed death sentence, but I let that go for now. "Sir Glomsby is the Dragon Lord's Champion. He will show you the encampment. I'm confident you will have much to discuss."

Sir Glomsby and I share a nod with each other. My nod is to ask if that's okay, and Glomsby's nod is to let me know that I handled everything well. I sigh with relief while Sir Glomsby and Bixel usher Sir Lakely and his guards out of the forge.

I turn to the rest of my companions and see that a terse argument has sprung up, only to be curtailed now that I have noticed it. Putter and Crat appear to be squaring off for a fight, but when I join them, they drop their combative postures.

"Is something amiss?" I ask them.

"Just wondering if you have any more need of me," Crat asks, adding, "*milady*," as an irreverent afterthought.

I regard him for a moment before answering.

"You've done all I've asked of you in half the time of another man. There is nothing more I could possibly ask of anyone. If you no longer believe in this cause, I offer you your wages and my gratitude for a job well done."

I reach for my purse, but Crat throws up his hands with a disgusted sound.

"Keep it. I ain't leaving as yet, and my money's safer with you than with anyone— including me. You and your Dragon Lord are as honest as Asphodel is crooked." He spins and makes for the door, tossing one last comment over his shoulder. "And when's the last time any of you saw honesty win in a knockdown fight?"

Crat stops before he gets to the door as if he's thinking better of it. He turns, takes off his hat, and bows to me.

"My lady," he says with genuine respect. Then he rises, tugs his hat down at a rakish angle, and saunters out the door.

"I don't trust him," pipes Jack, startling me.

"What are you doing here?" I ask her, shocked. Somehow, she'd hidden herself away in the shadows and watched things she probably shouldn't have. "You ought to be at the inn, sleeping!"

"I'm going, I'm going," she grouses, hurrying it up when she sees her father's angry expression. "It's about time I got a break, anyway," she adds cheekily.

I'm going to have to pay a little bit more attention to my apprentice. In the meantime, I am quite gratified to see that she is taking it upon herself to be where she needs to be— rather than where she *should* be— to gather the most information. I will have to have another talk with Ellison about her soon. But not tonight.

"I think young Jack has the right of it," Lakonius says,

stretching his enormous arms overhead as he yawns and talks at the same time. "I'm headed back. You?" he asks Ellison.

"I'll be along in a bit," Ellison replies, his attention absorbed by something in his hand— a rivet for what I believe to be the Dragon Hide armor intended for Sir Glomsby. "I've got to get this flush or the gauntlet will lock up against the pauldron if he pulls his arm back in line with his shoulder for a thrust."

I nod vigorously. "Right. Can't get your gauntlet caught on your pauldron," I say, though I have only the vaguest idea as to what he's talking about. Not a lot of knightly armor in a tinker's pack. "You get on with that, then. I'm going to bed," I announce.

"I'll walk you," Putter says, rousing himself from his seat by the banked forge fires.

"What? To the yard?" I ask blearily. I am truly exhausted, I realize.

"She's not going back to the inn," Lakonius says like that should be obvious, whilst hitting Putter on the arm. "She's going to Lord Dragon."

"Right," Putter says, nodding and shuffling his feet. I can tell from his posture that he's embarrassed, but hugely curious. Eventually, curiosity wins out over embarrassment in him. "Is that comfortable?" he blurts out, trying to picture... something.

Lakonius knocks him on the shoulder again. "Don't ask a lady that!" he chides.

Putter rushes to clarify. "Sleeping *on* him, I mean. He's awfully spiky as a dragon. I was just wondering how that," he grimaces and makes a crunching motion with his hands and fingers, "works."

"Putter. You are a horse's ass," Ellison states as plain as day.

"It's okay." I laugh and interrupt them before they can start arguing with each other in earnest. "Lord Dragon holds me in the palm of his hand— er, claw. It's quite smooth and warm and though there are no doors and no locks, I am entirely safe."

"Well, yeah, with a dragon holding you," Putter says with a whimsical smile. "I imagine that'd be right nice."

"It is." I smile back at him. "Imagine how well everyone in the kingdom would sleep with Dragon watching over them. Good night, good squires."

"Good night, Lady Jonara," they reply, bowing to me as I leave them.

Dragon's scales are still a livid red and the ground beneath him smokes gently with his heat. He opens his talon for me as I approach his head, his all-black eyes mere slits. I climb into his grasp and fall asleep almost immediately.

Yet, I don't stay asleep. The moon is high when I awake. I'm sweating. I push Dragon's talons open and slide out.

"Dragon, you're as hot as a flame," I complain. "Put your head in the river."

He does as I ask while I go look for a bucket. When I find one, I start sluicing cold river water over his body. Steam curls up from his hide.

"This is not good." I go back to his head. "Are you strong enough to swim?" I ask him.

He makes an indeterminate sound.

"If you can't swim, just dunk your body in the river. You've got to cool down."

He slides into the water, submerging his whole body, but leaving his head floating on top.

"You haven't eaten anything all day, have you?"

He blows some bubbles, making me laugh and alleviating some of my worry. If he feels well enough to tease me, the situation can't be that dire.

"Can you fish?" I ask. He lifts his head enough so that I can see him nod. "Then I think you should. Stay underwater. Cool down. Eat some fish. I'll go back to the inn tonight and sleep there."

He growls, and I know now why he hesitates.

"I'll be perfectly safe. I'll let Putter know, and he'll put guards on me," I reply. "Go. Meet me back here at dawn."

He moves close to me and I lean out over the water to stroke his snout. He hums something that sounds suspiciously like a familiar phrase.

"Yes, yes, you silly beast," I reply, smiling. "I love you too."

He slips under the water and is gone.

I trudge back to the inn. I find Ellison and Putter in the tavern, inform them that I'll be in my room this night while Dragon fishes, and mount the stairs. My head has barely hit the pillow when I hear banging on my door.

"Yes?" I call out, repressing my irritation. But just barely.

"Forgive me, milady!" Ellison calls urgently. "It's Jack. He's— she's gone."

24

I rise and go to the door, throwing it open. Ellison's face is pale and drawn. "What do you mean, gone?" I demand.

"When I got back to our room, she wasn't there. There was only this. Pardon me, milady, but I read it already."

Ellison hands me a piece of folded parchment. On the front, it says "*Lady Jonara*" in careful, yet childish block letters. I open it and read,

Crat figured out what I had around my neck. I tried to stop him, but he cornered me and took it. I'm going after him. I'm sorry I let you down.

Jack

"Oh no," I whisper.

"What was around her neck?" Ellison asks.

"The skeleton key for all the lockboxes!" I put a hand

to my head and force my staring eyes to see. Boots. Where are my boots? I find them and shove my feet into them.

"You made a skeleton key?" he asks, confused.

"No. Jack did."

"*My* Jack?" he nearly shouts. "When?"

"I had her make it in secret and keep it on her person, thinking it would be safest if no one knew it existed." A wave of guilt hits me. "I'm so sorry, Ellison. I thought no one would guess a skeleton key had been made, let alone that she had it. I underestimated Crat."

I tie up my laces and find my cloak, pushing past Ellison and the guards at my door without even stopping to put it on.

"What's this?" Putter asks as we race past him down the hallway. "Where are you going?"

I run down the stairs of the inn, trailing several people. Mistress Waverly appears from a small room on the first floor wearing her dressing gown, with Limond the bartender trailing behind her in an equal state of undress. Lakonius comes running down the stairs behind us, still pulling a shirt over his head.

"What's happened?" Mistress Waverly asks Ellison.

Ellison makes short work of explaining, and Putter makes a tisking sound, shaking his head as we strike out across the yard behind the inn and toward the stables.

"Crat wanted out," Putter admits. "He got a look at Asphodel taking the troll magic and said we didn't have a shot."

"But what's Crat going to do with that skeleton key?"

Lakonius asks. "It's not like he can rob the lockboxes and get away with it."

"He doesn't want the money, he wants his life," I reply. "Crat betrayed Asphodel, but he's hoping that bringing him the skeleton key will be enough to save him."

"Well, hang him then. What does it matter if Asphodel gets the key?" Mistress Waverly asks. "If we win, he'll be dead, and if we lose, he'll get the lockboxes anyway."

"Damn the key. I'm going after Jack," I answer. I enter the stables, but there is no groom in attendance. "Horse! I need a horse!" I yell.

"But *you* can't go, milady!" Mistress Waverly says incredulously.

"Why not?" I counter, pulling a saddle off the tack wall and throwing it over the freshest horse I see. "Who else should go but me?"

Lakonius stops my hands under his rough ones. "Jack's right clever, but without *you* what are we going to do?"

"You will prepare for battle," I say, turning to include everyone in this. "You don't need me any more. The men are assembled. Brave knights are here to lead, and you have a bloody *dragon* to kill the evil sorcerer. I'm going after Jack." I tighten the girth strap, put on the horse's bridle, and take the reins in hand.

"She's my daughter, milady. I'll go get her," Ellison says, trying to take the reins away from me.

"No, you won't," I retort, keeping the reins. "You'll go back to the forge this instant and finish Sir Glomsby's armor. I fear he'll need it by tomorrow."

"Er— daughter?" Lakonius interjects. "Don't you mean son?"

Mistress Waverly steps in front of me, halting my progress. "You don't mean to walk right into Asphodel's hands, do you? You are the queen on this chessboard. If you're taken, what of the king?"

"I have no death wish," I assure her. "I'm going to try to catch up to Jack before she makes it to his camp..." I look down and bite my lip. "And hopefully I'll be back with her before dawn."

"Why? What happens at dawn?" Limond asks.

"Lord Dragon returns from his fishing trip," I answer darkly. "He's expecting me to be on the bank of the river behind the forge."

"And what if you're not back?" Putter asks, his face blanching. "What do we tell him?"

"Tell him where I went." I give a weak chuckle and lead my horse out of the stall. "And tell him to bring an army."

I mount up and Ellison reaches to take my hand. His eyes are wide and desperate. He almost says something but settles for squeezing my fingers in his instead.

"I'll bring her back," I promise him. I dig my heels into my horse.

Behind me, I hear Lakonius asking, *"Here now, why did you call Jack your daughter?"* And Mistress Waverly remarking back, *"Are you just figuring that out now?"* as I speed away.

Though it is dark out, and the dead of night, I know which way to go. I may not have walked these exact roads, but I've studied all the maps of this area a dozen times over.

The thing about being a tinker's daughter is that you get quite good at reading maps at a very young age. Especially when your father has an abysmal sense of direction.

My father was always cheerful on the road, no matter how long it stretched before us. And it usually stretched longer than it should have because he invariably sent us the wrong way at least three times before we set off down the proper path. I can't claim the same cheerfulness for myself. Probably because I was the one carrying the pack. I quickly learned that if I wanted to get anywhere in under a fortnight, I had to be the one reading the map.

Later, as I grew in understanding of the world and its inherent pitfalls, I studied the maps to make sure we weren't accidentally going anywhere near the Forest of Woe. I got so good at avoiding that patch of dark and tangled land that I developed an almost preternatural sense of where it lay no matter what town we occupied.

And now I speed toward it with all haste. I can only pray that I will find some sign of Jack *before* the forest. I hope beyond hope that she has a modicum of prudence and quits her chase before entering that dreaded breeding ground of nightmares, though I know her character well enough to know that once committed, she will not give up. She is entirely too much like me.

Finally, I can see the tree line of the Forest of Woe ahead. It is a slightly darker smudge against the dark and starry sky. I must leave the road— for no road brings a traveler directly to the Forest of Woe— and as I do so, I slow my progress. I search for any sign of where she might have started toward the forest.

Fortunately or not, there is only one trail and it is easy to follow. Asphodel's army must have come this way, trampling down a new path into the forest that is nearly as clear as the main road. But path or no path, my horse knows well enough not to go in there, and he prances under me when I try to urge him under the smothering canopy of the trees.

"Woah," I coo, stroking his neck.

My horse and I stare at the monster-infested wood, trying to see into it. We both turn when we hear rustling in the leaf litter just beyond the line of impenetrable darkness.

"I'd promise you a treat to go in there, but since you're probably going to die, I don't want to lie to you. I don't have any treats."

My horse throws his head and harrumphs.

"Sorry, but there's a little girl in there and we've got to go get her, treats or no treats," I tell him.

My horse makes a terrible decision and obeys me. We enter the Forest of Woe.

Legend has it that there is a cave somewhere in this forest, and from that cave horrible creatures made of misery and magic are birthed. Or maybe monsters just prefer the darkness of the tree canopy, the ample rainfall, the plentiful game, and the bad reputation of the forest which affords them some solitude.

When the old king was still alive and in his prime, monster hunting was fashionable. The surest way for a knight to be invited to dine at the king's table at his fabled stronghold, the Ivory Spire, was for him to cut the head off something nasty and haul it to the spire's gates.

Either that or jousting. But with jousting, a knight

must face another knight, and there one's chances are locked at fifty-fifty. Monster hunting, however, could be done by one's retinue, and a lord or a knight wouldn't have to bother with the death and dismemberment that was a coin toss in jousting. During the late king's reign, monsters flocked to the Forest of Woe for a bit of peace and quiet. No one's stupid enough to come in here now.

Except me, apparently. And this gullible horse. I don't know its name, and I'm glad of that. It's best we keep our relationship strictly professional, seeing as how one of us (hopefully the horse) is likely to die.

The path is clear, though a bit less easy to follow in the darkness. My horse can see it better than I can, and I allow him to thread through the trees with more haste than prudence. We both startle at the skittering sounds of fleeing wee beasties in the scrub. I feel under my skirts for Dragonbarb, strapped as always to my thigh, and debate holding it in hand in case I'm set upon by something ferocious, or keeping it concealed in case I'm taken by Asphodel. To answer that question, I must decide what I fear more— the monsters, or Asphodel.

Before I can make a decision, mounted soldiers materialize before me on the trail.

I pull back on the reins and wheel my horse. Torches flare, and though I try to set out in one direction and then another, all my exits are blocked. I'm surrounded.

"I told you she'd be along after the girl," says a familiar voice.

I turn and see Crat astride a horse. He's holding the reins

of the horse next to him, atop of which is Jack, bound and gagged. Her eyes are red with crying.

"Traitor," I say icily. Crat shrinks at the word.

"And yet you turned my general," taunts another voice. "You *make* traitors. How dare you condemn them?"

I crane my head this way and that, looking for Asphodel in the dim golden pools of firelight. I hear his laugh, echoing.

"Show yourself!" I shout.

A black warhorse ghosts out of the leaves next to Crat's mount without making a sound. Astride the horse is Asphodel. His beauty startles me afresh. He sits taller than I remember and his skin glitters in the illusive torchlight, like it has been shot through with seams of mica, like a troll, I suppose. I've been fortunate enough to have never seen a troll before, but it appears my heretofore good luck has run out.

"Here I am, Lady Jonara," he says in his purring voice. The sound of it shivers across my skin.

"Let Jack go," I say.

"You are in no position to demand anything," Asphodel replies, his lip tilting up to show an inhumanly sharp incisor. "Though your unfounded arrogance amuses me."

"At least remove her bonds," I argue in a strangled voice. "Please. You needn't be cruel to a child."

I stare at him. He brings his horse alongside mine. This close I notice that his hazel eyes have turned green and that his skin has taken on an olive hue, like an ogre. He's still beautiful, though definitely changed.

"You should have been mine," he whispers.

I shake my head, confused. "That was never an option."

"Only because you were given to *him*."

I'm confounded. "As his *sacrifice*."

"If you were given to me, you could have made me a better man," Asphodel continues, barely hearing me. "But alas, I am never the hero."

"David doesn't need me to make him a better man. He already *is* one. *That's* why he's the hero," I retort.

Asphodel laughs suddenly, baring his unnaturally sharp teeth. "Perhaps I just need a sacrifice of my own." He pulls up on his horse and wheels about abruptly. "Bring them to camp!" he bellows.

My eyes lock with Jack's. Hands grab us both and we are pulled away from each other. I am encased in soldiers.

Though I struggle to peer through their hulking shoulders and meaty hands to find her, Jack is lost to me in the confusion.

25

We don't go very far, but we do go deeper into the Forest of Woe.

A clearing has been made, yet it is nowhere near big enough for two armies to come to blows. Though, from what I can tell, Asphodel doesn't have much of an army left. On an open field, he would have no chance at victory, but numbers don't matter as much in the dense forest where battalions don't have room to form.

Lacking an army, Asphodel has dictated the terms of the battle to suit him. He wants to fight David one-on-one. He thinks he can beat him, and I must admit, this tactic does give him a chance. I laugh bitterly when I realize that Asphodel has perhaps outmaneuvered me.

One of Asphodel's henchmen, for I refuse to call this unsavory collection of knaves *soldiers*, jumps down from his horse with unnatural alacrity. He takes my horse's bridle and gestures rudely at me to dismount.

The sun is rising, and though gloom remains here in the Forest of Woe, I notice for the first time that some of Asphodel's thick and lumbering henchmen have a green hue to their complexions while others have a chiseled or pebbly aspect. I guess that Asphodel must have bestowed troll and ogre strength onto a few of his closest guards.

I hesitate to dismount in order to test the henchman's patience. He grabs me about the waist and lifts me from the saddle as easily as if I were made of thought instead of flesh.

As he lowers me to the ground, I am close enough to see his face under his helm. He is much altered by Asphodel's enhancing magic. His jaw is squarer, and his neck is corded, but I still recognize him.

"Barth?" I gasp, dismayed. "Is it you?"

He makes a snarling face as he grumbles at me, and no more. He still regards me with the same derision he always has, but now it seems as if he were robbed of the power to tell me as much in speech.

Barth shoves me along toward a trio of tented pavilions that fly black banners from their top poles. He pushes me through the front flaps of the middle tent but remains outside. I am alone, though I see the shadows of bodies on the other side of the cloth walls. I look around the small space and see a pitcher of steaming water, a towel, and a basin filled with rose petals. Next to the basin is a chair, across which is laid an elegant red dress. At the foot of the chair are crystal-encrusted slippers, also red. Asphodel does so favor that color.

I pour the water into the basin and refresh myself before donning the dress. Unlike the last red dress Asphodel had me wear, this one laces up the front, and I need no assistance getting into it.

"Lady Jonara, are you decent?" Asphodel calls from the other side of the door flap.

I turn and brace myself for his audience. "I am," I reply.

Asphodel must bend nearly in half to fit his enlarged body under the opening of the pavilion.

"You've grown," I remark, unable to stop myself.

He lifts a corner of his mouth in an almost-smile. "I am prepared for battle," he replies quietly.

"By draining other creatures until they die? Tell me, has the ogre and troll magic reduced you to communicating in basic grunts the way it has Barth? Or do you punish Barth as you do everyone who serves you?"

I don't know why I'm baiting him. I only know it pleases me when I see him fumble around his thoughts looking for a way to reply.

"Reducing Barth to monosyllabic conversations was more of an act of self-defense than a punishment," he replies wryly. "And I am forced to drain monsters of their magic if I am to have any hope of defeating your Dragon Lord. But that's your fault."

"Mine?" I spit back at him. "How dare you blame any of your despicable actions on me?"

"He was nothing— a worm subsisting in a hole in the side of a mountain— until you came along." Asphodel walks towards me, and I must crane my neck to look up at him. "And since that day, I've been on the run. Hemorrhaging money and men. Every hard-won step I'd taken toward the crown, you have ripped away." He laughs with genuine humor and respect. "You are an utter *calamity* that has befallen me, leaving me a beggar with no chance lest I risk my very sanity by harnessing the darkest magic from the basest of beasts. You have nearly conquered me in a matter of days without casting one spell or drawing one sword."

I straighten my spine and regard him coldly. "If you accept that you are conquered, you should stop now before any more blood is shed."

He shakes his head. "No, milady. I cannot. I can never stop. For me, there is victory... or death."

He holds up his hands as I draw in a breath to tell him to die when he stops me with another smile. "And before you tell me to impale myself on the nearest pike, I feel I need to tell you that unfortunately, I cannot die that way. You see, I am cursed, milady. A Dragon Lord might be able to do the job, but I'm not even quite sure. We will soon find out if that's the case, but in the process, many lives will be lost. Unless..."

"Unless what?" I prompt.

"You win my war for me and give me the crown. Then, maybe I will find some peace." The look on his face is desperate and, well... tired, really. Asphodel is exhausted in his very soul.

"All you want is the crown?" My voice is tentative.

His eyes fall. "All I want is *out*." He shrugs. "Maybe if I win instead of lose for a change, this will all be over."

"What will be over?" I ask him.

It seems like he almost knows what to say, and then it slips away from him.

"What would you have me do?" I am at a loss.

Given his stature, his eyes must lower to meet mine, but still, it feels as if he is raising his eyes to mine in supplication.

"Break David's heart," he requests quietly. "Tell him you love me. That you always have. That your time shared with him was a lie."

My jaw falls in disbelief as I digest what he's asking.

"That will kill him."

"Precisely."

I laugh in his face. "I would never—"

"If David dies, none can oppose me. I will become king and no one else need die." He looks at me, hopeful. "You can save Sir Glomsby, Sir Lakely, Mistress Waverly, Putter, Lakonius, Ellison." He pauses and his voice roughens with feeling. "Jack. Your father. Prince Bixel. I will spare your friends and family. I will spare your entire army. All you need do is tell David that you are mine."

I back up until my legs hit the chair. "I can't," I say. As I use the chair to steady myself, I feel Dragonbarb buried in my discarded dress.

"You *can*," Asphodel urges, nodding. "Break his heart. Kill him quickly. It's best for everyone." He frowns in thought. "I would make a great king, you know."

I shake my head to clear it, not believing all that I am hearing. "Sir Lakely expounded on your talents the first time I met him. At that point, he still supported your bid for the crown. Later, he came to me in horror at what you'd become." I meet Asphodel's eyes to keep his gaze away from my busy hands. "You are clever, resourceful, and driven. But I don't know from one meeting to the next which version of you I am going to encounter. This one— who seems honorable, even likable— or the evil man who steals people's names." Behind my back, I grasp Dragonbarb firmly. "That's why you would make the worst king our land has ever had. My answer is, no. Not because I'm too squeamish to break David's heart, or too selfish to let him go. My answer is no because beneath it all... you are a villain."

Asphodel doesn't look angry, or surprised. He looks relieved. He moves back so he can see me in totality. He looks me over carefully, taking in my proud stance and my sweeping skirts.

"You are everything I hoped you'd be, milady," he says, bowing deeply.

Seeing my chance, I lunge forward with Dragonbarb in hand while his eyes are down.

He rights himself before I am half the distance to him and catches my wrists in his easily. His eyes harden. He squeezes my wrist painfully until I drop Dragonbarb.

"And, unfortunately, everything I expected," he informs me, though his expression falls.

He picks up Dragonbarb. I fight him as he grabs my arm and hauls me out of the pavilion, but it's like being tied to a landslide. When my incessant tugging and kicking becomes irritating to him, Asphodel simply lifts me up with one arm and carries me to one of two stakes that have been driven into the middle of the clearing.

Already shackled to the other stake is Jack. She is wearing an unbound white shift of the finest, purest linen. It is very like the white dress I wore when they gave me as a sacrifice to Dragon. Jack is gagged and her hands are hoisted above her head by chains. Asphodel pushes me against the other stake and presses my arms up over my head. I hear the shackles click above me, though I can't feel much difference between the iron and his grip. Asphodel leans his body against mine to pin me in place. His mouth is close to mine.

"I'm well aware of your ability to pick locks. So, you leave me no choice."

I feel something like a bite in my side. And then warmth, followed by a cooling wetness that pools its way down my side and the top of my leg. I am suddenly weak. I hear Jack scream behind her gag, but everything is becoming hazy. I look up at Asphodel, gasping for breath to keep my eyes open. My lungs don't seem to work as well as they used to.

Asphodel steps away from me, holding Dragonbarb up so I can see my blood on it. He's stabbed me. He walks over to Jack's stake, and before I can murmur, *no don't*, he stabs her in the stomach. Scarlet ribbons of blood christen her white dress. She falls limply in her bonds in a matter of seconds. Asphodel comes back before me.

"Would it *really* have been harder to say you loved me?" he asks quietly.

I try to answer, but something thick and salty spills out from between my lips instead of the words I'd intended. Asphodel steps back to avoid my mouthful of blood.

He calls over his shoulder. "Bring the last of them!" he orders.

Barth and a few other ruffians run off and come back a moment later, dragging two chained ogres behind them. One of the ogres looks vaguely female, and the other is certainly an ogre child.

The female shelters the child with her body. Though my

head tips on my neck as if my bones were starting to melt, I force my gaze forward as I watch Asphodel cast a spell. He closes his eyes and mumbles strange words.

One of his arms shoots out toward the mother ogre and her child, and there is a distortion in the air, like looking through a convex pane of glass. The distortion grows between his hand and the cowering pair. The mother and child fall to their knees. She tries to shield the child, but they both weaken and tumble to the ground, shriveling up like cut grass in the sun.

Asphodel holds out his other hand toward me and Jack. I brace myself for the worst as the rippling air hits me.

I feel stronger. I pull myself up on my chains. I look around, confused. Asphodel takes a deep breath. He comes towards me, staggering slightly. I know something is desperately wrong because he looks pleased.

"What'd you do?" I ask him, my voice croaking in my throat.

The look on his face is like that of a drunkard. He stumbles against my stake, nearly fainting. Something falls to the ground, but I can't see what it is. Then Asphodel giggles, which is disconcerting. "You my dear, are now… invisible."

I glance down at myself. My red dress has a darker streak down the front of it where blood pours out, and though I can see myself, I can also see *through* me. I gaze up at Asphodel, and over at Barth, but they are solid. I look over at Jack and notice that she is like me. I can see through her.

"Jack!" I yell.

She does not react.

"You can see all, but none will see you, or hear you, but

me," Asphodel continues. He seems to be regaining his strength.

"Why are you doing this!?" I ask him. "Why not just kill me!?"

"Because I may need you," he replies. "If your Dragon Lord somehow manages to defeat me, my enchantments over you will lift with my death— both the invisibility and the spell I am using right now to keep you alive. You will be revealed to him, so he can watch you die."

"You're evil," I whisper, but he continues as if I hadn't spoken.

"He'll come to realize that you were bleeding to death while he fought me. It will break his heart to know he might have saved you, and that will kill him. Which means that I will be dead... but I will still have won."

26

A small group of Asphodel's non-green ruffians runs into the clearing, yelling, "They're coming!"

Asphodel spins away from me. "My armor," he barks, striding quickly to one of the pavilions with the black banners.

"Jack," I call as soon as he is out of earshot. "Jack, wake up!" Her head bobs in response, and I can hear her mumbling a little, which is some comfort. We can hear each other, and she still lives.

I look up at my chains and try to suss out the lock on my wrist cuffs. There's no easy pin to be pulled out this time. I'd need a key, or a very stout hairpin, neither of which I have. I look around frantically, but I'm shackled to a stake that's driven into the middle of a clearing— there's nothing *around* me. Except...

Asphodel dropped something a moment ago, I remember, and in his magic-drunk state, he didn't notice.

I look down and see Dragonbarb's hilt miraculously sticking out of the ground. The blade has cut completely into the sod, but the hilt still sticks upward. It is not a yard from my left foot. I poke my leg out and knock it over. When it lies flat on the ground, I put my foot on top of the hilt and drag it over to me. The effort has left me winded by the pain from my wound, but I can't stop. Now I must figure out how to get it all the way up to my wrists without eviscerating myself on that unimaginably sharp blade.

I slide off a red slipper and start to feel around the hilt with my bare toes, looking for a secure way to grip it. As I do this, Asphodel's men pour into the clearing. They form a circle facing outward toward the forest. I can hear shouts among the trees, and the sound of many men coming through the underbrush at a run.

Asphodel strides out of his tent wearing black armor. I tuck the blade under my foot to hide it from him as best I can. He watches me while he takes his position at the center of the ring.

From the tree line, many voices are raised in a unified battle cry. Asphodel's ruffians bellow back at their hidden adversaries. And then utter chaos ensues.

Bodies hurl themselves from the cover of the trees, swords drawn, teeth bared, and legs pumping furiously as they rush headlong into the fray. The first clash of swords is a storm of shrieking clangs that pierce the ears like lightning does the eyes. Guttural howls quickly follow, and the banging, grunting, ringing, and screaming of the battle suddenly surround me on all sides. Men fly through the air, thrown this way and that by the magically enhanced members of

Asphodel's inner circle, and those that aren't enhanced grapple with the desperation of the outnumbered.

No one can see me, and so my stake becomes a place where men pummel each other as they fight hand to hand. They bump into me and feel me, but in the panic of battle, it matters not to them. I try my best to shield myself with a raised knee or a deftly placed kick, but as I do so, Dragonbarb is trampled underfoot and kicked hither and yon.

At first, I'm just trying to not get stabbed or cut in half by a wild swing of a sword. Then I realize that if I don't pull myself together, I'm going to lose Dragonbarb altogether in the shuffle. Though the battle has only been raging for minutes, the noose is tightening around Asphodel's men and everyone is being pushed closer to the center. Where I am.

I wrap my toes around Dragonbarb's hilt and squeeze it tight. A man fallen onto his knees in front of me offers a convenient step stool, and I plant my other foot on his back as I swing myself upside down from my chains.

Several men stop, noticing the moving chains and the knife that is apparently levitating, and of course, the man I am using as a step stool notices weight pressing down on his back.

I pull down hard on my shackles and tighten my belly to get my legs over my head despite the agony this causes. Instead of focusing on the pain, I distract myself by thinking of how I would look to these warring men if I weren't invisible. They'd see my skirts completely flipped over and my exposed ass blazing like the sun in the sky as I pass Dragonbarb from my toes to my fingers.

As soon as I've made the transfer of Dragonbarb to my hand, I relax my belly and my legs fall back to the earth. I hang from my shackles for a moment, letting the pain wash over me. When I can finally raise my tear-filled eyes again, I notice Bixel. He stares in my general direction with confusion, though he does not look directly at me. Rather, he has noticed the moving chains and the levitating knife, and they have caught his attention.

"Bixel!" I scream, though uselessly. He is mere paces away from me, but he can't hear me, and in the next moment his attention is engaged in a fight.

Bixel quickly takes up his opponent, but he is only keeping the man busy while Sir Glomsby finishes off the man he was fighting. The two of them are fighting back-to-back, with Putter (holding the dragon banner high) throwing the odd kick or thrust here or there. Although Bixel is enormously brave for coming into the very worst of the battle, it appears he's no swordsman. He guards Sir Glomsby's back admirably, though, while the armored knight does the actual killing for the both of them. Sir Glomsby finally gets around to Bixel's man and while he does so, Bixel turns his attention back to my stake.

He stands for a moment, staring at Dragonbarb hovering in midair. He points to it, knowing something is amiss, but alas. Before he can put all the pieces together and come to help me, his attention is diverted to protecting himself and Sir Glomsby again.

A blare of trumpets catches everyone's attention.

Sir Lakely comes riding into the clearing on a dappled grey warhorse. His greatsword drawn, he leads a charge that breaks the ring around the clearing and sends men screaming into the woods.

After Sir Lakely's entrance, most of Asphodel's men have been decimated or have run off, but those that remain bear the green and vaguely sparkly skin of the ogre-and troll-enhanced. The one who engages Sir Glomsby now does so with familiarity.

"Glomsby!" bellows Barth.

"Barth?" Sir Glomsby asks, dismayed.

Barth doesn't reply. Instead, he charges.

Sir Glomsby faces Barth in his Dragon Hide armor. He tilts a shoulder down and lets Troll-Barth roll over him. Troll-Barth springs to his feet again and comes running back at Sir Glomsby with unnatural speed. They clash with a mighty force and tumble off into the forest, knocking down trees as if they were tender shoots.

Bixel goes running after Sir Glomsby, and I lose sight of them. I look up at my numb hands and try to coax my fingers into spinning Dragonbarb around so I may slice through the chains. I get through one side of one link and let out my held breath.

A hot wind presses down on the clearing from above.

A comet descends, burning gold and red. It lands with a boom that buckles the earth and sends out ripples of cracked soil. Men are flattened to the ground by his coming as if pressed down by a hand from above. When he rises from the crater of his own making, he stands twelve feet tall.

This is neither Dragon nor David. Part man, part dragon, this is the Dragon Lord in his full and terrible glory.

His golden-scaled skin still smoking, the Dragon Lord

curls his red wings into his back where they disappear. He flexes his shoulders and breathes two plumes of smoke out of his nostrils as the scales on his skin widen, grow, and transform into proper armor. Horns extend from his head and wrap around to form a helmet.

"Asphodel!" the Dragon Lord booms.

His voice pounds into me like a fist. I nearly drop Dragonbarb. I manage to catch the hilt with my fingertips and then I begin the exhausting process of trying to get it back into position while my hands lose ever more feeling above my head. My body grows weak with loss of blood, and I must blink my eyes to keep them focused. A few insane men try to attack the Dragon Lord and he kicks them away from him like he was beheading daisies with his foot.

"Asphodel!" the Dragon Lord calls again.

"Here!" Asphodel answers.

Though I am much occupied with my positioning of the blade, I look over to see a suit of black armor, grown in stature to match that of the Dragon Lord's, striding forward.

The two giants face each other. Asphodel draws his greatsword.

The Dragon Lord cocks his head. Then he lifts a hand, places his fingertips on his breastplate, and presses down. His dragon scales move aside and he pushes straight through his breastbone. The Dragon Lord reaches into his own chest, grabs hold of a piece of his broken heart, and pulls out a greatsword of flaming black metal.

He holds the smoking sword aloft. The sunlight catches the diamond edge of it, and it sparkles like ice rimming burnt metal. Written down the flat side of the blade, in glowing fire letters, is the sword's name. *Calx.*

The hole in his chest closes and the Dragon Lord points Calx at Asphodel. "Where is Jonara?" he demands.

"Dead," Asphodel replies from behind his black helm. His mailed hands flex over the pommel of his sword anxiously as he rocks from foot to foot in a fighting crouch. "I killed her."

The Dragon Lord's shoulders round in sadness and Calx's point dips momentarily before the Dragon Lord lifts it again.

"Then you have killed all mercy in me," the Dragon Lord responds. He draws in a deep breath and exhales fire.

Asphodel holds up a hand, his fingers twisted into a magical sign as he speaks words of power. The column of fire splits in two and goes around Asphodel, leaving him unscathed.

The two warriors rush each other, their swords meeting in a blindingly fast barrage. I look up at my hands and hack away at my chains with refreshed urgency. Though I've damaged multiple links and left a series of nicks and cuts up and down the length of the chain, the cuff is preventing my wrist from bending enough to get the right angle to cut all the way through. I let out my held breath, take another, and try again.

The fight moves closer to my stake. Asphodel glances over at me. He registers what I'm doing and his eyes blaze, but he can't do anything to stop me, not without betraying my presence. It must be hysteria that makes me grin at him while my hand continues to saw away furiously.

Distracted by my temerity, Asphodel barely turns his head back in time to stop a thrust. He stumbles to the side and the two warriors circle each other. Asphodel begins to taunt the Dragon Lord.

"What are you going to do if you actually win?" Asphodel asks. "Jonara was the one with all the ideas. How are you going to rule?"

"I don't mean to rule," the Dragon Lord answers. "When I kill you, I will leave this place."

The Dragon Lord rushes forward, and they exchange a series of blows before Asphodel pulls back to circle again. He is breathing hard, while the Dragon Lord looks fresh.

"You're just going to *leave*?" Asphodel demands. "You may as well let me be king then."

"Killing you... is my quest."

"To avenge her?" Asphodel asks. "It won't bring her back."

The Dragon Lord rushes in with a snarl. The blows are hard and fast. I look up at my chains. There are dozens of cuts in them. In some places, only the tiniest sliver of metal holds them together. I give up trying to cut through and just pull down. I yank on them with all my weight and all my might. I yank until my head feels light and I'm gasping for breath. Finally, I hear a *ping*, and I drop to the ground as my chains break. Asphodel sees me free myself, and he moves the Dragon Lord away from me with a burst of energy. I am too weak to chase.

I know Asphodel will not let me get near enough to the Dragon Lord to touch him and alert him to my presence.

I stumble over to Jack. My limbs are clumsy. I fall and get

back up, trying not to accidentally kill myself on Dragonbarb. I make it over to her and cut her down. I put my ear to her lips. I feel the faintest whisper of her breath against my cheek. I tear off the hem of my dress and press it against her wound.

Though my attention has been focused on my own predicament, the battle still goes on. The few combatants that remain have given Asphodel and the Dragon Lord a wide berth, but at the fringes of the clearing, I can see Sir Glomsby still fighting Barth, and Bixel guarding his back.

I manage to crawl to Bixel and punch him in the leg.

"Here now!" Bixel exclaims, looking about. I wave Dragonbarb under his nose. He sees it and narrows his eyes.

"Jonara?" he asks, his eyes wary. "Is that you?"

I punch him again.

"Right," he says, rubbing his shin. "I'm guessing Asphodel cast an invisibility spell on you— *don't* punch me again if I am correct."

I don't. Instead, I grab his arm and pull him towards Jack. He can't see her lying on the ground, so I carve the word "Jack" in the ground next to her head, and direct his hands to her wound.

"What am I touching?" he asks as I press his hands down.

I write "stab wound" in the ground with Dragonbarb. Bixel's face hardens with anger.

"She's nearly dead. This is going to *hurt*."

He closes his eyes and lets out a long breath that is filled with sparkles. He blows the sparkles all over Jack, and the color comes back into her ashen cheeks.

I check her wound and see that it is nearly healed, but now Bixel looks sickly. He crumples to the side.

I grab onto his arm and steady him as he lies down next to Jack.

"That was awful. I need a little rest now," he says, speaking toward the general direction of my face. "If anyone looks like they're about to lop off my head, stop them for me, will you? I'll be worthless for a day or two."

I look up at Asphodel and the Dragon Lord fighting each other to the death and feel torn. I can't leave Bixel here unable to defend himself. Yet, I also can't let the Dragon Lord kill Asphodel. If he does, I will die.

Asphodel begins to stumble, unable to weather the onslaught any more. The Dragon Lord wounds Asphodel in the leg, then the shoulder, and finally in the side. Asphodel drops his sword, but the Dragon Lord doesn't finish him off. Instead, he steps back.

"Pick it up," the Dragon Lord says coldly. "I'm not done with you yet."

Asphodel starts laughing. He stands up and limps over to his sword. "It is me who is not done with you yet," he taunts.

Asphodel is shrinking. Whatever magic enlarged him and made him strong enough to fight the Dragon Lord is beginning to wane. I can feel myself weakening as well. Blood starts to pour out of me afresh as the spell that is keeping me alive begins to dissipate.

"You're no king," Asphodel says. Then he does something unexpected and runs at the Dragon Lord with a surprising burst of speed. The Dragon Lord lifts Calx just in time and runs Asphodel through.

"No!" I scream, though only Asphodel can hear me. I stand up to run to them, but my legs won't work. I take a few clumsy steps and fall to the ground.

The horned helm on the Dragon Lord's face retracts into his skull. His body shrinks until he is back to normal size. The armor stays, but instead of the Dragon Lord, his face is David's again. He's crying. I pull myself closer to him, trying to get near enough to touch him.

"You're nothing," Asphodel growls at him.

David lets go of whatever thread he held to keep himself together. "And you are just a character in a *book*!" he shouts back. "None of this is real! *You're* not real!"

Asphodel's face freezes. His eyes grow wide with horror. "That's impossible. You're lying!"

"The book is called *The Chronicles of Lucitopia*. People like me, from the real world, come here to play a part. You are just a character in a book, Asphodel. And I hope that knowing it gives you no peace, as I will have no peace without her."

Asphodel sits down heavily on the ground, nearly bumping into me. He has a lost look on his face. He holds onto Calx, the blade still protruding from his chest, and casts about like a sleepwalker awakening in a strange place.

"I knew there was something wrong with this world. I always *felt* it wasn't real," Asphodel says to no one in particular. His gaze drifts over to me and he smiles. "Shall we die together, then?" he asks me.

"Don't," I plead, but too late. Asphodel throws himself further onto Calx. His eyes go blank, and he is dead.

David startles, his head turning toward me. He sees me

now. His eyes find mine, and the shock I see there is quickly replaced with dismay. He launches himself across the few feet separating us and lifts me up into his arms.

"Jonara!" he gasps.

I want to tell him that it's okay and that it doesn't hurt that much. It's actually excruciating, but there are worse things— like the way he probably feels right now. I wish I could take away the regret I see in his eyes, and tell him that it's not his fault. And that I wouldn't change a thing.

Well, except dying, of course.

But I can't tell him any of that for I can't even keep my eyes focused on his face, and though I wish his face was the last thing I saw in this life, it isn't, because he puts me down.

I can't believe it. That ruddy monster. He's put me down while I am probably drawing my last breath.

Sir Glomsby has carried Bixel over, and Bixel is waving his arms about and shouting something that I can't hear because I'm bloody dying, while David is frantically scrabbling about for something...

Then all I see and feel is white nothing. Like a blank page.

I pull air into my starved lungs and nearly drown on something salty. I cough painfully. I taste blood. Disturbingly, I don't believe the blood is mine.

"You're alive," David whispers, though he's practically drowned me again. In his blood. Ew. But effective.

I feel him holding me. I am alive.

27

The next few hours are something of a blur.

Dragon's blood can heal any wound, even for a person at death's door, but it doesn't do so immediately. As I recuperate, I am aware of armies kneeling before David, hailing him as king. I see the faces of friends hovering over me with worried frowns. I even see that gullible horse. I'm glad he made it, though he appears to have a new rider now.

Mistress Waverly arrives in a flurry of orders. Lakonius has brought my father. My da cries a bit, but only because he's happy I'm on the mend.

David changes into Dragon and holds me in his claw while he gives his blood to all the wounded, whether they fought for him or against him. He means to be king to all the people, not just to those who love him— though, after hearing of his kindness, there will be few who do not. Except possibly Barth. He's alive and recovering because of David, but some people you can never win over. And there are some people I'm not so sure I *want* to win over. Crat ran before the battle even started. Sir Glomsby sent men after him, but I'm hoping we never see him again.

When David has given enough blood, he changes back into a man and carries me inside one of the pavilions. He dons a pair of black leather breeches I'm quite sure belonged to Asphodel, but I'm not going to mention that since I rather like them. David sits next to me, his eyes round with fear.

"I think I'll be all right," I reassure him, looking into his grave face.

"Physically, yes, I know," he replies. "But—" he lets out a sharp breath. "Jonara. Did you hear what I said to Asphodel? When you were invisible, were you close enough to hear...?"

"Ah," I say, nodding and looking down. "You're worried I heard you telling him that he was a character in a story." David nods. "I did."

"Jonara. Listen to me." He holds my hands in his and speaks urgently. "My life story, your life story— it's all stories, isn't it? Stories we tell ourselves are real, but when you think about it, what's really real? To me, what's real is this moment right now." He takes a moment to gather his thoughts. "I forfeit my chance to go back to my world when I chose to tell Asphodel what he was, which means that now *this* is my world. Here. In Lucitopia. With you."

"David," I say, cutting him off before he can get himself tied in knots. "I *know*. I've known most of my life."

"Wait. What?" David asks, bewildered.

I smile at him. "My Da told me when I was six. He said it was the only way he could stay with me."

"W— your *father*," he repeats, incredulous.

"Yes." I look down at our hands. "He told me I was a character in a book. He said that it was a rule that he couldn't tell me, or he would have to stay in Lucitopia. I was so young, and he never used the name again, and I forgot it. Well, nearly. Then, I heard you say it."

David sits back, still staring at me in utter shock. "So, you've known all along?"

"Not about you. I didn't know you were from the same place he was from. You said *Lucitopia*, and then I remembered. And then I forgot again. Did Bixel put a spell on me?"

"He did," David says, narrowing his eyes.

"I was about to tell you, but that spell, it muddled my mind."

"I could kill him," David says half-jokingly, but still quite miffed.

"No," I say, shaking my head as I touch his face. "I can't be angry at anyone or anything right now. I'm too happy."

"Me too," he whispers, leaning close to me.

"My liege?" my father calls from outside the tent, interrupting us. "Is it all right if I come in for a visit with our girl?"

"Will we never be left alone?" David whispers.

I laugh silently and call out an answer for him. "Yeah, Da, come on in," I say.

My da comes to my bedside and bends down to touch his forehead to mine, as is our custom.

"Come and sit here," I tell him, clearing my throat so I don't cry. I'm unaccountably emotional at the moment. "David and I were just talking about how you and he are from the real world."

"Oh, you too, son!? That's right nice!" He takes the seat on the other side of my pallet. "I'm from Surrey, what parts do you hail from?"

"Ah—Rhode Island?" David says uncertainly like he's not sure he should be having this conversation.

"An American! You do a fine accent, then," my da says heartily. "Never been to Rhode Island. Spent some time out west, though, with the wife before she passed. We were never blessed with children, so we traveled quite a bit. Beautiful country, Colorado."

"Yeah," David says, still blindsided. He holds up his hands and then massages his temples. "Wait. You told Jonara that she was a character in a book when she was a small girl?" He turns to me. "And it didn't bother you?"

"I was too young to understand," I reply, thinking back. "It bothered me a bit later when I was— what twelve? Thirteen?"

"Eleven, actually," my da reminds me. "You came to me asking if the real world felt any different from this make-believe one."

"And you said it didn't," I remember.

Da smiles at me. "Then you asked me how I knew the difference if they felt the same."

"No," I correct, wagging a finger at him. "I said that if they felt the same, how could you know that the world *you* came from was the *real* one? What if *it* was just another story?"

"My clever girl." My Da pats the back of my hand. "When I saw you crying by the side of the road," his eyes get misty, and so do mine, to be honest, "you became more real to me than anything else in the world."

I roll my eyes, but only so I don't start crying in earnest. "Stories have always been more real to you than anything," I grumble.

"Quite so," he confesses. Then, he perks up. "Did you see the fairy, love?"

"Yes," I admit reluctantly.

"Ha!" he says, slapping a knee. "I told you fairies are real! That was my quest here in Lucitopia, after all. Helping Oberon, the king of the fairies."

I sigh and look at David. "I never believed him. Now he'll never let me live it down."

"Did I ever tell you that story?" my Da asks.

"Only a hundred times, Da," I say tiredly.

"Well, I've never heard it," David says, grinning at me while I groan. "And I love a good story." David's eyes warm as he looks into mine.

"So you do! Jonara— *she's* a good story, all right." My Da mumbles to himself for a moment, getting a kick out of David's play on words. "Say, when are you two going to get married and give me some grandchildren, eh?"

28

The big day comes upon us in a tumble.

Mistress Waverly was essential to the planning, as she knows the ins and outs of social graces. The ceremony is to be held among the fairies per David's request. He wants Bixel to stand up for him, and I couldn't deny him that, though it raised many objections and quite a few arguments about who was going to be allowed to cross whose territory without anybody killing anyone else. Fairies don't get along with other magical folk. Scratch that. On the whole, magical folk don't get along with other magical folk. I don't even want to start about what a nightmare the seating arrangement turned out to be.

I will say that though I had been vaguely aware of how the different species in the land held varying opinions of each other, I had no idea what a political nightmare it was to invite both the Eldest of the Trolls and the Centaur Lords to the same function—though not inviting either one of them would have been tantamount to a declaration of war.

There was also the grim realization that nearly all the magical folk across the land were now suspicious of any human (or in David's case a half-human, half-dragon) king after their hideous treatment by Asphodel. David and I thought it best we invite everyone and hang the awkwardness of it.

Still, as this day approached, I couldn't help but feel as if I were putting out fires left and right. The Brownies refused to set foot in "hoity-toity" Fairyland; the Queen of the Elves made her mistrust of anything non-elf clear (apparently, she'd nearly been overthrown when she was a small child); and even David wondered about my sanity when I invited the ogres. But I *had* to. After seeing first-hand how Asphodel had abused them, I felt as if they needed some recognition from a human-ish king, if only to let them know that we aren't all like that. I invited the Ogre Whump, which I'm mostly sure is their version of a leader, or at least the one they all obey because if they don't, he or she whumps them on the head.

I haven't told David I've invited the Unicorns though, because I'm afraid he'd put his foot down about that. I had Jack set up some troughs of purest spring water and salt licks of the finest quality, and hopefully, the miserable creatures will be satisfied with a quick drink and a lick and run along before they decide to gore half our guests to death.

When I arrived in Fairyland with my retinue to prepare a section of the Sacred Oak Grove for what is sure to become a debauched scrum, Oberon, King of the Fairies, greeted my father with a hug and a broad smile that was damp with tears.

It was touching to watch the two of them reunite, though you couldn't imagine an odder pairing. Oberon is an impressive creature with enormous iridescent wings. The King of the Fairies is almost as pretty as his wife, Titania, but quite frankly nothing is more beautiful than the Fairy Queen. Hmm. Except for maybe the Elf Queen, Isfin. I was told her name means "snowlocks", and she is quite possibly the most eye-blindingly stunning female imaginable.

But I've decided that it is pointless to dwell on the beauty of some of my guests. I've got to get into this great big dress, and I'll be hanged if I'm going to spend the whole morning fretting about how thick my waist is in comparison to females that are— in point of fact— inhumanly slender and capable of fitting into one of my sleeves.

David has never complained about the shape of me. In fact, on several occasions, he's mentioned that in his world my figure is quite coveted. I am, apparently, built like something called a J-Lo. I am both *ripped* and *bootylicious*. Now, quite frankly, "ripped" sounds painful, and "bootylicious" calls to my mind someone eating boots, but David insists the only thing it calls to his mind is knocking them. He has yet to explain that euphemism to me, but I'm assuming it's something musical, for upon mentioning "knocking boots", he started singing a song. But he got... er... distracted and never made it past a few bars. I'm assuming the song is quite romantic based on his reaction to it. I'm eager to hear this rap poetry that is so popular in his world, but he says there is no way to recreate it here. He says it comes from the 'hood, and not the kind you wear, which I still have not figured out yet.

"Milady, may I enter?" Jack asks from outside the entrance to my pavilion.

"Come!" I bark. Jack enters, but I start berating her before she can speak. "What are you doing in here? You've got to stay by those troughs. If the Unicorns show up, I need a virgin girl—"

"They've shown up," Jack says, white-faced.

"How many guests are dead?" I ask woodenly.

"None as yet," Jack says, shaking her head, "but you'd better get out here."

"Right," I say, hiking up my golden skirt. It weighs a bloody ton. Probably because it's made with real gold thread. What a terrible idea. "Grab the train for me so I don't throw my back out," I tell Jack as I pass by her on my way out. "Did you inform Lord Dragon?"

"Er—no?" Her face widens contritely. "You told me not to tell him!"

"Don't tell him about the ruddy *Unicorns*," I say like it's obvious, "just tell him we have to *start*!"

"Right!" Jack says, dropping my anchor of a train to run off and fetch him.

"Get Oberon out there first! He's the one who got to mumble the words!" I shout after her in the most undignified manner imaginable.

"Might I assist you, Lady Jonara?" inquires a dulcet voice. Isfin, the Elf Queen, has materialized at my elbow in a decidedly disturbing way. Like a cat, she is.

"Your Highness," I say, curtsying deeply, though my

thighs protest the weight of my dress as I do so. "I fear we must begin the ceremony a bit earlier than expected. Certain guests have arrived that make tarrying unwise."

Isfin's sculpted face tightens in a charming smirk. "That could describe a full two-thirds of your guest list, though I'm assuming you are referring to the Unicorns. I applaud your bravery for inviting them."

"Oh dear. You've seen them?" I ask, popping up to scan the crowd anxiously.

I see that the Ogre Whump is already eating— good— he won't be tempted to gobble up a few Sugar Sprites. The humans are following Sir Glomsby's orders and have scattered about the gathering, making polite conversation. The Redcaps are busy untying everyone's shoes and pulling the pegs out of everyone's chairs, so they are too occupied with their pranks to try to anger the Unicorns. And as far as I can see, the Merfolk are keeping to the river that Oberon magically turned into saltwater for the occasion.

"I smelled them," Isfin says, interrupting my perusal. "They are keeping to the salt licks for now, and no one else knows of their arrival. If it's of assistance to you, I can go and quiet them, though I believe your young handmaiden has done well with them on her own."

I skip past the unsettling part where the Elf Queen told me she smelled the Unicorns and go straight to her offer.

"I would be grateful if you would assist in any way, Your Highness. Jack— my handmaiden— is terrified of Unicorns."

"Smart girl," Isfin says. She stifles a laugh and tips her

head in assent. I wonder how old she is. For a moment, she seems younger than me.

"I will find you after the ceremony," she says.

I drop down into the lowest curtsey I can manage. "Your Highness," I say reverently as she takes her leave.

Blast. Now I can't seem to get back up.

"Are you stuck down there?" Bixel asks.

"Get a winch," I tell him. Two curtsies and my thighs are done in. I'm not going to make it through the night. "And then get *up* there, for the *love* of *all*. I want this over with before one of the Trolls sits on someone."

Bixel hauls me to standing. "You're doing great, you know," he tells me as he passes me off to my Da. "I think this is the longest any of them have spent in each other's presence without bloodshed. I'm surprised none of my relatives have started killing each other."

"Don't hold your breath," I say, giving my corset a sharp tug. "The Unicorns just got here."

Bixel's eyes widen. "Oh, bloody hell. I'll make it quick." He runs off in a dither to the front of the gathering and signals to his father to begin.

The crowd settles down as soon as Oberon steps into place, and the whole party goes silent. The Sirens accompanying the Merfolk begin their song. I find David's eyes over everyone's head, and it's like we're suddenly alone. Dressed in white and gold, he is a marvel.

He'd asked me if I wanted to wait to get married so I could have a big ceremony with all the pomp and circumstance of a queen. I told him I intended to get married like the tinker's daughter I was— rushed and at a tavern. We were married two days after the battle, by Limond the barkeep who happens to be a Druid, surprisingly. I was still recovering from my wound and could barely get out of bed long enough to hold up a glass with everyone at Mistress Waverly's Inn. Which suited me and David just fine, as we retired immediately and didn't leave our bed for days.

I asked him if he was sorry that his family could not be here with us, and he told me he had never known his father, and his mother had passed before he came to Lucitopia. There was no one he cared deeply about in his world, and that I would have to provide him with the family he never truly felt he'd had. We eagerly got to work on that in short order, and I for one hope to have a child as soon as possible. I just pray that at twenty I'm not already too old, though David insists that in his world he and I would still be considered practically children ourselves. Which is utterly ridiculous, of course.

And now, a month later, he is going to make a queen out of me with all the pomp and circumstance that I had eschewed for our wedding. I know from one look at David that he is thinking the same thing I am. Though we stand in an enchanted oak grove where the trees are said to be sentient, the wine was pressed from star berries hundreds of years ago by the Elves, where Sirens sing to us as we clasp hands, and we kneel in front of the King of the Fairies to give our vows of service to the people, our wedding at the Waverly Inn, where we were served bread, cheese and beer, and were married by a half-drunk Druid, was immeasurably sweeter than this coronation.

David and I must look down at the sacred ground to

control our laughter. Luckily, Oberon takes our bent heads for reverence and begins his benediction of our kingship and queenship.

We rise to give our parentage. Neither of us has birth parents to stand up for us, but Prince Bixel stands for David, and my father, Phillip of Surrey, friend to Oberon, stands for me. Our guests are relieved that the lineage part of the ceremony is so brief. Usually, this is the part where everyone nods off for a while, but David and I are crowned within moments.

My coronet is a solid gold circlet with only one jewel perched atop a single peaked prong that arrows up from the center of my forehead, so that the gem may catch the most light. When Oberon is done anointing my forehead with oil, he places the crown on my head and our guests gasp.

The jewel is the largest, most perfect diamond ever seen. Mounted high in a raised setting of my own design, the Heart Diamond catches even the dim light of the Sacred Grove, and throws a halo of rainbows around me. The only crown I ever want to wear is the light of David's love.

David's crown now grows from his skull, a latticed weaving of gold and horn. As his crown branches up from his brow, his fangs extend down until his diamond incisor sparkles. Our guests buzz in awe as David parts his shirt at the front, and delves his hand into his own chest to retrieve Calx.

The burning, diamond-edged sword emerges from his chest with only a few dabs of blood. David holds Calx aloft, flames leaping high, and everyone present kneels to chant as one,—

"All hail the Dragon King!"

I see a white flash at the edge of the sacred grove and look to see that even the Unicorns have bent their knee. David sheathes Calx back in his chest and takes my hand.

I lean toward him and say, "You should either wear black or no shirt at all."

He laughs and whispers in my ear, his lips brushing against my cheek, "I know which you'd prefer."

I turn my mouth toward his ear, the ghost of his lips still on my cheek. "I invited the Unicorns," I tell him, and then I dissolve into a throng of our guests before he can yell at me.

I am giddy while I duck away from David, imagining the delightful ways he'll make me pay for my deception later, when I hear the whispers.

"I think he'll make a great king. But that doesn't change the fact that Asphodel will be back."

"He always comes back."

I turn about the press of bodies I've entered to see who's spoken, but taller people with broad shoulders seem to cut me off from seeing faces. As I jostle through the crowd, I hear more snippets and whispers.

"Enjoy the light while it shines. The darkness will return."

"He always comes back."

Desperate now, I push my way past a large elfin man. As I make my way around him, Isfin sees me and extends a hand. The elf guards around her glide back with elegant tilts to their heads. They seem smaller now, when just moments ago they seemed to tower so high and broad that they were a veritable wall.

"Your Highness," I say, tipping my head instead of bowing. We are equals now.

She tips her head back at me, accepting my status. "Your Highness," she says back.

"I overheard you speak of Asphodel," I say hurriedly, "and forgive my forwardness, but I must tell you that there is no way for Asphodel to return. I saw him die."

Isfin smiles sadly, her eyes falling. "If only death of the body were enough," she replies quietly. Her eyes snap back to mine. "Asphodel must die body and soul, and though your Dragon King has spared us for several of your human generations to come, he will be back in my lifetime. Unfortunately."

My eyes find David, talking merrily with Sir Glomsby and Bixel, who have their hands entwined. Past them, I can see white hides flashing among the trees. The Unicorns are there, but no one is screaming and running from them. I think I see Jack out there. She and the other maidens are playing with them. I can hear their laughter and put my fears aside. I decide that today is a day for joy.

I take Isfin's cool hands in my warm ones. "Asphodel told me that he had lived many lifetimes, but David told him something before he died that I believe killed his soul. I saw the light go out of him."

Isfin looks down at our entwined hands. She smiles shyly at me, and says, "I hope to one day call you a friend. For an elf, friendship is earned over decades. If you live a life as long as that— which you might with your dragon love's blood to keep you young and healthy— longevity will grant you one fell thing. And that is that someday, my almost-friend, you will see that Asphodel will return."

Isfin drops my hand, and the elves disappear in the oaks.

"Have I missed the elves?" David asks behind me.

"Only just," I reply turning to him.

He frowns, mirroring my troubled expression. "What is it?" he asks.

I banish Isfin's parting words from my thoughts and encircle my arms around David's neck. "Is it over yet?" I ask, groaning.

He laughs and kisses me, his eyes growing tender as he withdraws. "No, my love," he replies. "We've only just begun."

ALSO BY JOSEPHINE ANGELINI

THE CHRONICLES OF LUCITOPIA

Illustrated Girl

Ensorcelled

STARCROSSED SERIES

Starcrossed

Dreamless

Goddess

Scions

Timeless

Outcasts

Endless

WORLDWALKER SERIES

Trial by Fire

Firewalker

Witch's Pyre

THRILLER

What She Found in the Woods

For more information please visit:

josephineangelini.com

Printed in the USA
CPSIA information can be obtained
at www.ICGtesting.com
JSHW022131271124
74439JS00002B/2

9 798987 832172